Betrayal by an Irish Rose

BETRAYAL BY AN IRISH ROSE

Margaret Nyhon

Willow Press

*How could something so beautiful
come from such poverty?*

*'Only my Irish Rose,' said Lord Albert,
of the one he loved so dearly.*

Contents

Introduction

This family saga begins in Ireland, in the mid to late 1800s in the counties of Cork and West Cork.

In County Cork people were moving away from farming to the industrial sector. This was the beginning of the Industrial Revolution. In the little town of Ballydehob, between 1779 and 1841 the population swelled to around 20,000 people. Many industries grew rapidly, especially in mining, among them coal and slate. Carboniferous slate was found on the southeastern coast of Cork where it occupied a considerable area. This slate was mainly used for roofing, flooring, worktops and headstones.

The poorer people were drawn to the coal mines. With this industry's growth, owners pushed the workforce to the limit to improve profits and to expand. This added extra danger to the workplace, especially in the coal mines. Because owners wanted to produce as cheaply as possible, the workers were paid by how much coal they produced, rather than by the hours worked. Some workers took their whole families underground to get as much coal as they could. The poorer families lived in sod mud huts, some with no windows or furniture, as poverty in Ireland was widespread. Some of the luckier families had cottages supplied by the mine owner but they were often two-roomed to house six to eight people, from which the owners would collect rent.

The work day started early in the morning, with families having to walk several miles before they reached the mines. They would then work up to twelve hours a day, six days a week. The only day off was Sunday. Those children that attended Sunday school sometimes received basic training in the alphabet, counting and Bible stories; this was their sole education.

Once they reached the mines, they would be lowered into the pit on the end of a rope into total darkness. The only light was from the miners' candles. These were made of tallow, the fat of animals, as it was the cheapest light. The miners had to supply their own candles. Because of the cramped conditions in the mines, small children were used to push or pull tubs or large baskets of coal on sleds along narrow roadways. It was hot and stuffy in the mines and workers wore little or no clothing while they worked. This included women and girls as well as men and boys. Water was always present in the coal mines, as it seeped through the rocks from above, so flooding was always on the workers' minds. Rats or mice were forever present as they fed on the crumbs left behind by the workers.

1

The Plight of James and His Family

James was the second son of Daniel Nyhan. Daniel was a tenant farmer in Drinagh, but because the farms were small they could only support one wage, so as the children grew older they had to find work outside of the farm. The farm land was owned by absentee landlords mostly who were rich aristocrats that resided in England. They collected their land tariffs, and most of the time they had no connections to, or compassion for, the plight of the Irish tenant farmers. All they were interested in was the rent. At this time there were jobs in the mining sector, so James left the family home and went to work in a slate mine in Ballydehob. While working there he met and married Margaret Foley in a little church in Schull.

In 1845 the face of Ireland changed forever. This was the beginning of the great potato famine. It was brought about by the invasion of a tiny potato-killing fungus. This turned the potato black almost overnight making it inedible. The counties of Cork and West Cork were among the worst-hit areas. This was where many rural poor lived; their staple diet was the potato, and they had become dependent on it. Because many families grew potato crops, their income was destroyed and so was their main food source. The Irish soil was ideal for growing the potato. An acre and a half of land planted in potatoes could provide a family of six with enough food for a year. The land produced more income from potatoes than wheat per acre.

Most of the large productive farms which produced wheat were owned by the English Protestant gentry. The Irish farms produced the wheat, which was then sent to England. Even when the people of Ireland were starving, the gentry exported their wheat to England, thus leaving the Irish people to starve. This stayed in the minds of the Irish people for many years. The attitude of many British intellectuals was that the crisis was predictable and not unwelcomed, so as to curb the high birth-rate of the Irish.

The tenant farmers struggled to provide for themselves and their families, as they had no income. Because the peasantry was unable to pay the rent, this resulted in hundreds of thousands of Irish tenant farmers and labourers being evicted from their lands during the years of crisis. Each year between 1845 and 1849 the potato crop was almost completely ruined by blight, which sparked off a decline in the Irish population that lasted half a century.

From a population of 8.5 million, over 2 million were driven by panic and desperation to leave Ireland forever. Families were split as Ireland's future looked dismal. Thousands of people died of starvation and fever.

James, Margaret and their seven children were not exempt from Ireland's pain so they sailed across the Irish Sea to Cornwall in England. James found work in the tin mines in Camborne. They were provided with a home as long as he worked in the mine. He worked alongside many of his countrymen who were also forced to leave their homeland to put food on the table to feed their families. James worked hard to provide for his family; it was not easy as the wage barely gave them enough to live on. For four years they struggled, then tragically Margaret died, at the age of forty-two. She left behind Kate, sixteen; Mary, fifteen; Norah, fourteen; Daniel, twelve; Margaret, eleven; Patrick, nine; and Julia, six. This was a huge tragedy for the family. No-one knew that it was starvation that killed Margaret, as she went without food to feed her family.

As James looked back over his life, he and Margaret were like any young lovers. They spent many hours in each other's arms making love; this took their minds away from the outside world. This was where they felt safe and happy and reality was replaced with dreams. But, of course, with these actions came consequences ... that of babies. Because they were devout Catholics as were most Irish people, birth control was not an option — it was forbidden. Margaret was with child within months of marriage. This is what happened in Ireland; the people were so poor their only chance of happiness was between the sheets in each other's arms making love, enjoying those exciting moments that brought a little joy to their lives. They could not be denied this! This led to the Irish having large families, which was frowned upon by the English gentry, as they could see the Irish population exploding. At that time, most of England was Protestants, and to see the Catholics multiplying like they were, became a worry. So, when the potato famine happened, the English were not sympathetic. As they had not suffered poverty like that of the Irish, they did not understand that these people deserved moments of happiness together in each other's arms.

Their first-born was a little girl they called Kate. Life was a struggle as James's pay was minimal and the potato crops were still non-existent as the blight had gone into the soil, thus still destroying the crops, but at least they were able to survive. Many of their family members and siblings had been lost to the famine. The following year Margaret was with child again. This was a reprieve for James as while his wife was with child, he could perform his marital duties without fear of another child, other than the one growing within Margaret. With another baby on the way, things were going to get harder as this meant another mouth to feed. Their life outside work and the family was non-existent; it was only the home pleasures that brought them a little joy. Their second child was a little girl whom they named Mary. The struggles kept coming as people were dropping like flies, dying of fever and starvation. No sooner had Margaret stopped breastfeeding Mary, she found she was with child again. This pattern went on for the next four years when they had Norah, Daniel and Margaret. James had to work extra hours to put food on the table for his growing family. They had a reprieve for a year, then Patrick arrived. The only way to stop adding to the family was to refrain from the only thing that gave them the greatest pleasure. But three years later Julia arrived. Now they had a family of seven children to feed, and life became a struggle; they couldn't survive in their present situation. Men were being laid off as the slate mining took a dip and James feared he would be next. How would they survive if this happened? This was when they left Ireland for England; they had no other choice.

James could not afford to give up work because his wife had died, so Kate, who was the eldest child, had to become the mother figure to keep the family together. Mary had seen her family suffer through hardships all her life and decided this was not going to be her life, but beggars could not be choosers. She managed to get a job housekeeping with another family who had lost a mother, leaving behind three young children. She was paid very little, but a little was better than nothing. She didn't have a choice, they needed the money. Because Mary was a beautiful-looking girl, the widowed father became infatuated with her and she decided after three years she had to leave before it got out of hand. Meanwhile, a heartbroken James worked at the tin mine to provide for his family. All his pleasures were now gone, and life was one of survival for him and his family.

Mary was on the train to London. The only money she had was enough to get her cheap lodgings for two nights, so she had to find a job as soon as possible. As she was walking from the train station to find lodgings, she was amazed at how many poor people were on the streets begging for food. After walking the streets for an hour, she came across lodgings where she could afford a room with just a bed; all other facilities were shared with the other lodgers. Mary was the beauty of the family — it was that beautiful thick red Irish hair that was her standout feature.

She still harboured a deep resentment of the English gentry for sending their wheat back to England thus leaving the Irish to starve. These thoughts never left her, she was so bitter towards them. She had heard of the rich gentry clubs in the city so decided to find out where they were, and if one was close she would go and have a look at these awful men. First, she had to find a clothing shop in the hope she could shoplift a dress without getting caught, so she could look more presentable. She would come back and pay for it as soon as she earned some money. She knew it was wrong to do such a thing, but desperation drives people to take desperate measures.

After committing her dishonest deed, she went back to her lodgings and put on her new dress. She had chosen an orange colour to match her hair, which she let down so it flowed around her neck. She looked a real beauty. Now it was time to find one of these clubs that was nearby. She walked with her head held high until she saw a line of flash carriages driving towards a large building in the square. This must be one of them, she thought, and positioned herself so she could have a look at these men as they alighted from their carriages. Several of the men called out to her but she ignored them. She didn't think they looked any different except for their smart suits and the little bags they carried. Suddenly, she was grabbed from behind. She felt frightened — she didn't know who her attacker was as she couldn't see him. A middle-aged gentleman who was alighting from his carriage saw the young lady in distress and yelling for help, so he came over and hit the attacker with his bag, frightening him off. Mary was shaken and began to cry. The man put his arms around her to comfort her and led her to his carriage. What a beautiful soul, he thought. Her red hair fell around her shoulders and as he leaned over, it touched against his cheek. He reached for a handkerchief so she could wipe the tears away from her eyes. He had forgotten what it was like to feel his heart touched again. Who was this young lady? "Thank you for helping me," said Mary, letting him know she was grateful. "Please, tell me who you are," he said. "I am Mary, I have come to London to find work." "Maybe I can help you. Do you like gardening? I am looking for someone to care for my gardens." Mary told him she would be grateful for any sort of work, she was a strong girl. As he had to attend a meeting at the men's club, he asked her to come to this exact spot the next morning at ten o'clock and he would pick her up in his carriage. Mary thanked him again. "I will see you tomorrow," she yelled. This brought a grin to his face; such beauty, such innocence. What an interesting young lady, he thought, I will look forward to tomorrow.

Mary went back to her lodgings and climbed into bed. She was tired from her train journey and still a little shaken from being attacked. But to be offered a job on her first day in London, that was a bit of luck. She was pleased she could lock her bedroom door from the inside, as all night she could hear banging outside her room. She didn't sleep very well as she kept one eye on the door. What would tomorrow bring? she asked herself. She rather fancied the idea of being a gardener ... but where?

The next morning when Mary woke, she went to the bathroom to bathe. As she made her way along the hallway, she bumped into a young man who had the same idea as her. He suggested they share the bathroom. As soon as he spoke she knew he was Irish. He was a fine specimen of a young man and very pleasing to look at. They struck up a conversation as they entered the bathroom together. Mary asked him if he would guard the door while she got undressed and bathed. He agreed if she would do the same for him. She poured the water from the jug into the tub, then she started to undress. He watched her shed her clothes and his eyes never left her body. She was one beautiful girl, and this was the first one he had seen totally naked. Strange things were happening to his body, which left him excited and wanting to hold her. He undressed and climbed into the tub with her. She felt his arms encase her, the water was warm, he was Irish, she was alone in London, so they sat with their arms around each in the warm water. Mary felt his manly body touching her soft skin and she snuggled into him. Was this an invitation for him to take her? It was awkward in the tiny tub, but where there is a will, there is a way ... and they tried their darndest! There were squeals of delight. Here were two total strangers who knew nothing about each other, not even names, but who were fellow Irish. The squeals from the bathroom did little to please the people lined up waiting to bathe. "Hurry up in there," they called. They dried each other, both touching parts of the other's body. They hadn't finished, so they wrapped their towels around themselves, gathered their clothing and ran to Mary's room. They lay on her bed desperately wanting to finish what they had started. He cupped her breasts in his hand and she fondled his manly parts and again the excitement became too much so they writhed around in the bed until the deed was done. God knows when she would meet another handsome young man to make love with, especially an Irishman. Mary loved the feeling of togetherness; she felt complete. They lay in each other's arms until she remembered she had an appointment at ten o'clock. She jumped out of bed to get ready. They both agreed to meet that night, as she had another night paid for. Still no names were exchanged, as they had more exciting things to do other than talk; that would happen tonight. All she knew was he was originally from County Kerry in Ireland and, like her, was seeking work in London.

Mary yelled goodbye as she raced off to meet up with the man that had come to her rescue the previous afternoon. True to his word, his carriage was waiting for her. As he alighted he greeted her and asked how she was. "I'm fine, thank you," she answered. "Where are your belongings?" he asked. Mary was taken aback as she didn't know she was meant to bring them. "We are driving out to the countryside; I will supply you with lodgings. Can you go and pick up them up?" he asked. With this, Mary asked him to wait five minutes and she would go and fetch them, hoping he would still be there when she got back, but he wasn't going anywhere. He would wait forever for her. She had not left his mind last night and he fretted she wouldn't turn up this morning. He could still feel her beautiful hair brushing his cheek, and the warm message it sent him.

Mary tried to find the young man from this morning but he was not to be found; he must have gone out for the day. She wanted to let him know she wouldn't be back tonight. She grabbed everything — there wasn't much — and put it in her bag. She had to go in case the man with the carriage was leaving. She badly needed the job, so she ran down the street to his carriage. "Is that all you have, Mary?" he asked her as he helped her into the carriage. "Yes, I don't have many belongings," she answered. "My name is Lord Rothchild. It will take a good two hours to my home." Mary could not believe what she had just heard. Did he say Lord? She asked him to repeat his name again. "I am Lord Rothchild but you may call me Lord

Albert, as you will be part of my household." Poor Mary, she was stunned. This was like a dream; would it fall apart before it began? They chatted away as they drove out of the city into the countryside. He learned that Mary was Irish, which accounted for her beautiful red hair. This would be a bit of a shock to his fellow gentry, who didn't care much for the Irish; they were the menial workers who supplied them with a living, a good one at that. The gentry were landowners who could live entirely from rental income or at least owned a country estate. But Lord Albert was more than just gentry; he was a lord as well, thus holding a higher rank than the gentry.

He loved her Irish brogue. This young lady was something else, and he felt an instant attraction to her. Mary was taken by the countryside and kept telling him how beautiful everything looked. She was so excited; never before had he seen such excitement over very little really. He loved the way she expressed her feelings and let them be known. This made him think she was a very excitable young lady. Mary took notice of the signposts and they were approaching Oxshott, which was still in the Surrey county. They drove a little further, then suddenly veered off to the right down a gravel driveway. There before Mary was a huge mansion surrounded by lovely gardens. She could not believe her eyes. To the left of the mansion was a large glass building. "What is that?" she asked. "That is a conservatory, my dear. That is where I grow all my plants. You will be working in there on wet days." As they pulled up at the front entrance, Lord Albert said, "We are home now, what do you think?" Mary couldn't find words to express herself; she was overcome with disbelief. Tears streamed down her cheeks. Surely this was just a dream. She blinked several times but it wouldn't go away, it was still there. "Oh Lord Albert, this is beautiful. Are these the gardens I have to look after?" she asked. "Yes, Mary, you are in charge of my gardens as from tomorrow." Mary took his hand and thanked him for giving her a chance. "I will work hard and keep everything beautiful for you, I promise," she said. He didn't doubt her for one moment.

As Mary alighted, Lord Albert helped her down, and she turned and reached for her bag. Suddenly, she felt it being taken from her by a man and he took it into the home. "Put Mary's bag in the pink room," Lord Albert instructed the butler. "The pink room, are you sure, sir?" "Yes, you heard me, the pink room." Did this mean she was sleeping in the home? She expected to be in the servants' quarters out the back. "Come, Mary, the butler will show you to your room. I will meet you in the dining room in half an hour for lunch." "Follow me, miss," and he led her down a hallway into a separate wing. He opened a door and told her that was her room. "Through the door off the sunroom is your bedroom." Mary thanked him. She stood and looked around. She had her own sunroom furnished with white furniture; what would the bedroom reveal? She walked through into the bedroom and there was a four-poster double bed decorated with a canopy and lace curtains. Why was she put in here? she asked herself. She was only a servant, she didn't deserve all this. Off the bedroom was her own bathroom. Mary was bewildered; it was almost too much for her to take in. Who did it belong to, was it his daughter or his wife? She had so many questions to ask Lord Albert.

The time had slipped by and half an hour had passed. She quickly washed her face and brushed her flaming red hair, then set forth to find the dining room. At the end of the hallway stood the butler who was waiting to show her to the dining room. As she walked in, Lord Albert was seated and he rose as Mary entered, then sat down when she was seated. She thought this was back to front; she was the one who should have stood while he was seated. "Is everything to your liking, my lovely?" he greeted her. He couldn't take his eyes off her. He was infatuated with her hair; never before had he seen such beauty. "Yes, thank you, Lord Albert, everything is perfect. Whose room am I ...", but before she could finish, he interrupted. "No questions before lunch." With this, the cook brought in a trolley with breads, meats and fruit and laid it out on the table. Mary was shocked as she thought back to only two days ago, when all she had to eat was a piece of bread. In fact, yesterday she hadn't eaten at all because her lodgings had taken all her money. But then a smile came over her face when she remembered it was only this morning she had made passionate love to a lovely young Irishman, one of her own, and she didn't even know his name. She always knew in her heart she would definitely marry an Irishman ... but not a poor one!

"Come, my lovely, eat up," he told her. Poor Mary, she didn't realise how hungry she was until she had seen the food, so she tucked in and ate a hearty lunch. He realised then that she couldn't have eaten in a while, as he watched her fill her empty belly. "When do you want me to start?" she asked. "Tomorrow I will take you for a walk around the gardens and explain everything. Just spend the rest of the day wondering around or resting. We will discuss pay and board later. I will see you again at six o'clock for supper." With this, Mary thanked him for the lovely food and told him she was so grateful for his kindness. He smiled at her; never before had he met anyone who expressed out loud how they felt at that very moment in time. She had no traits of the fine-bred English ladies who never revealed their thoughts, especially out loud. Mary excused herself and took her leave.

She walked out the entrance door onto the patio and then made her way to the gardens. The roses were blooming and the fragrance coming from them was heavenly. She had never felt this happy, only when she made love to the young Irishman. She held out her arms and pretended to be dancing with him around the garden, then she stopped and picked a yellow rose and put it in her hair and continued dancing. This was all being observed from a study window in the left wing of the mansion. Lord Alfred couldn't take his eyes off her; she seemed so happy, she was beautiful, her flame-red hair was flying unruly around her face sometimes hiding her facial features, then when she added the yellow rose, she had become part of nature itself. Such raw beauty he had never seen before. All the money and land he owned could not measure up to what he felt, watching this unfold before his very eyes. He had seen many beautiful English women, but this was something spectacular, this was his very own Irish rose. He was disturbed by the doorbell — it was the butler wanting to know something but he waved him away, telling him to come back later. He didn't want this picture set in motion to have an ending, but as he had experienced, everything came to an end. As he watched from the window, his past came flooding back. His wife had left him because he couldn't give her children. They both blamed each other, but neither knew the real cause. It was easier to part and let the blame lie with whomever! She walked out with nothing, thus explaining why everything was still as she left it. Mary had been put into his ex-wife's living quarters, which was why the butler questioned Lord Albert's decision to put her into that room, as it had not been used for seven years. He couldn't understand why Lord Albert instructed him to make it liveable again, after he came home last night. The butler wondered if this was going to be the next lady of the mansion. His master had not bothered with any other woman before now. It wasn't as if they weren't available; plenty were waiting in the wings, but he seemed to have lost interest.

Suddenly, Lord Albert saw Mary doing cartwheels on the lawn, so unladylike, so impulsive. Her dress fell over her head and all he could see was the poor girl's bloomers. Were they still worn? No English child would wear such an item of clothing, but then Mary was not English, she was Irish. He laughed out loud as she looked so funny, thus bringing the butler rushing in and they both laughed together. Neither had seen this behaviour by a young lady. This was the best entertainment Lord Albert had seen in years and it was unfolding in his very own garden. No amount of money could buy this entertainment ... it was priceless!

Next, Mary walked over to the conservatory and as she slid the door open the heat rushed at her. She stood and looked at the strange plants, most of which she had never seen before. How could she look after them if she didn't know what they were? It was so hot in here, she decided to take off her dress and she threw it outside on the lawn. Then she tried to read the names of the plants but they were so silly; fancy calling plants those names. Suddenly, Lord Albert could not see his Irish rose from his window. Where had she gone? He came outside to look for her, then he thought he could see someone in the conservatory so made his way over. What on earth was her dress doing lying out on the grass? He looked in and he could see her walking around in her bodice and petticoat. What is she doing now? he wondered. She was full of surprises. He didn't want to embarrass her so he walked away. He couldn't risk losing her, what would he do without her? When Mary had sorted things out in her mind, she stepped outside and slipped her dress back on. She made her way back to her room and lay on her big bed.

While she was lying there, a strange thought came to her mind. What if Lord Albert came to her room and wanted to share her bed? This thought had not crossed her mind until now. Mary had heard of these things happening. How would she feel? If she loved her job and could live like a princess, it would be a small price to pay. She knew what it was like to be poor and without food, but she had left that all behind. If at times she had to make sacrifices so she could have a better life, then she would. Nothing was going to stand in her way ... nothing!

At six o'clock Mary made her way down the hallway to find the butler waiting to take her the dining room. She had brushed her hair and tidied herself, but she was still wearing the stolen dress. "Good evening, my lovely, have you had a nice afternoon?" enquired Lord Albert. "The best," Mary answered with a giggle. He asked her why she was laughing. "I'm worried how I am going to look after the plants in the conservatory when I have never seen them before." Lord Albert assured her she would manage. He poured himself a wine and asked Mary if she would like one. "I've never tasted wine before." "Then you must try one, my lovely." With this he poured her a glass. "Cheers," he said as he held his glass in the air. Mary did the same, not quite sure what this was all about. She took a big gulp and choked, thus causing Lord Albert to laugh. "No, my lovely, you just sip it like this," and he showed her. She managed it much better after being shown, although she continued to screw her face up with each sip. Perhaps it would taste better next time, she thought. When the evening meal was laid out on the table, Mary's eyes boggled. She had never seen so much food. "How many people are coming to dinner?" she asked. "There are just the two of us, my lovely." Her mind drifted back to what her father and siblings would be eating and tears welled up in her eyes. She had to look away and try to blink them back. Lord Albert took particular notice of her reaction to the food, then realised she was just a poor Irish rose who had probably never seen so much on a table. How could something so beautiful bloom from such poverty?

Mary tried a little of everything, then picked up her bones and nibbled around them making sure nothing was left to waste; she was like a little dog with a bone. Lord Albert was intrigued. She must know what it is like to starve; perhaps that has been her life? We of the gentry could learn a lot from this humble race of people, he thought to himself. "Tell me about the potato famine," he said. This was a controversial subject with Mary. She told him how she despised the English gentry who grew wheat in Ireland and imported it to England while her people starved. She told him how she felt and what she saw, all the time tears streaming down her face. "With every day came the desperate need to survive, otherwise we starved, froze to death or died of a terrible disease," cried Mary. He could see she had suffered. "Come here, my lovely, no longer will you have to suffer. I will never let you go back there." He took her hand and touched her beautiful hair; his heart was torn and he felt sad within himself. Unbeknown to Mary, Lord Albert owned many of the largest wheat-producing farms in Ireland and he was part of the English gentry that pushed for the wheat to come back to England during the famine. He would have to keep this from her; if she found out, he would certainly lose her. He couldn't bear this thought.

They retreated to the drawing room to discuss Mary's hours of work, her pay and her board. She was to start work at eight o'clock and finish at five o'clock with an hour for lunch. The weekends would be her own. He offered her a starting wage of £2,000 a year, and out of this each week came £10 for food and lodgings. Mary couldn't believe the amount of money she would be left with, she was thrilled. "Are you happy with this, my lovely?" he asked. She went over to him and hugged him. He could feel her soft red hair brushing his cheeks again, remembering this feeling from their last meeting. It had lingered this long and now he could hold on to this feeling again. "Mary, I want you to wear the dresses in the wardrobe. All that is in your room is now yours." "But who did they belong to?" she asked. "It's a long story, which I will explain another day, but not now," he answered. Mary thanked him for a lovely supper. He told her the cook would have breakfast ready for her in the morning. "I will be up and we will walk the gardens and I will tell you what I want done," he told her. With this, Mary left and retreated to her quarters.

Meanwhile back at the London lodgings the young Irish lad was knocking on Mary's door. He had been four times but there was still no answer. He went to the office to see if they knew where she might be, but they told him she had paid for two nights. When he told them they had arranged to meet, but there was no reply, they went together to her room. The door was not locked and when they went in the key was on the bed and her belongings were gone.

They looked around but could find no clues to what might have happened to her. He went to his room and lay on his bed and cried his heart out. Where had she gone? He so wanted to spend another night with this lovely Irish lass. They said at the office her name was Mary. That was all he had, a name, but one he would never forget.

2

The Start of a New Life for Mary

Mary bounced out of bed and put on a plain dress, one of her own, and plaited her hair so it wouldn't blow around her face while she was working. She was so excited, this was the start of her new life, one that would never see her starve again. She would work hard to please Lord Albert and to keep her job. She could post money back home to her father and siblings, as she would have plenty to spare. After breakfast she went out to the garden shed where Lord Albert was pottering away. "Good morning, Lord Albert, I am excited to be starting work today." "That is good, my lovely, we will start here. I will explain all the tools to you." Mary had never seen such a huge workshop before. How would she remember everything? She would have to listen carefully and remember one word for each tool. After they had gone through all the tools, they walked out into the rose garden and he showed her how to dead-head the rose bushes with the pruners. There were hundreds of bushes, so this would keep her busy for a couple of weeks. As Lord Albert was walking back, she noticed he walked with a slight limp.

Mary loved working with the roses. At the beginning of each day, she would select a rose and put it in her hair for that day. Unbeknown to her, Lord Albert spent most of his day watching her from his study window as he did his bookwork. He smiled each morning when he saw her select a rose and place it in her hair. He would play a guessing game with himself trying to pick which colour it would be today. She was such a happy soul; in his heart he loved that very little brought her such happiness. This raw Irish rose had more passion than any cold English rose.

A month had passed and Mary loved her job. She was now cutting the grass verges around the gardens. This was a huge job and she was on her knees most of the day. One morning as she stood up she felt sick in her stomach. This continued each morning. Things weren't right in her body; she had missed her monthly cycle. It was only then she realised she was with child, and she remembered back to that morning with the young Irishman. Did this mean the end of the job she loved so much? Was starvation going to creep back into her life? Starvation, that dreaded word, she hated it as much as she hated the English gentry who left the Irish to starve.

At the end of the working day Mary bathed in warm water to relax her body and take away the tiredness. She sat and brushed her hair making it shine like gold. It was her crowning glory. Today she had picked a yellow rose and brought it home with her; she would wear it to supper. As she made her way down the hallway she was met by the butler. "You look lovely tonight, Miss Mary," he said as he escorted her to the dining room. When Lord Albert looked up and saw his raw Irish rose, something happened to him. His breath was swept away, this was beauty beyond imagination. He would give up everything to own this vision that stood before him. He stood up as she sat down. He poured them both a red wine and they had the customary 'Cheers'. "You look positively radiant tonight, my lovely," he greeted her. Strangely, Mary felt her cheeks flushing. Was it the wine? They talked and ate and in-between times had another wine. This was not at all like Mary, as she usually struggled with the first one, but the second glass just seemed to ease its way down nicely. After supper they retired to the drawing room and talked about work. It was going to rain tomorrow, so she would learn how to grow seedlings in the conservatory. As Mary got up to leave she walked over to Lord Albert and hugged him, as she felt affectionate tonight. As soon as her hair touched his cheek he took her in his arms and held her. There was no resistance from Mary; she needed all the reassurance she could get at this moment in time, as she was frightened about the future that lay ahead for her. He released her and took her hand, leading her along a hallway where she had never been before. This must be where his bedroom is, thought Mary.

Lord Albert led her to his bed and sat down beside her, nestling his cheeks into her hair. This was the most beautiful place on earth; the sun shone from above and lit up his heart. Never before had he experienced such a peaceful, heart-warming place to be. He stroked her hair and kissed her forehead, telling her how beautiful he found her. "You are my beautiful Irish rose," he kept muttering over and over again, and Mary saw tears in his eyes. She excused herself and stood up and let her dress fall to the floor. She undid her bodice and took off her bloomers. There before him stood a statue of gold, a priceless piece of art. Her flame-red hair fell down around her breasts. Tears rushed to his eyes, never before had such beauty befallen him. With all his wealth, he could not purchase what stood before him. "Come, my lovely Irish rose," and he lay her down on his bed. As he undressed, Mary noticed he had a wooden leg. Was that why he limped a little? she wondered. He apologised to Mary as she looked at him, so she put her hand to his lips and asked him to bed her. She was so afraid for her future, a wooden leg was not even a consideration. She needed to be loved, to feel safe, anything to take away the fear of starvation and poverty. He was gentle with her and when passion took over he bedded her tenderly. He buried his face in her hair; it was so silky, he was so infatuated with her, never before had he known such happiness, such warmth and generous of giving, expecting nothing in return. Mary felt loved, just what she needed to take her mind off other things. She hoped she had made Lord Albert happy. She felt she should ask him. "Did I make you happy?" she asked. "My Irish rose, I have tears of happiness. You brought me such joy, more than I could have asked for. No amount of money could buy me this that I feel in my heart. Poor as you might be, Mary, your heart is so rich. I have learnt more about feelings since I met you than I have in a lifetime and it is you who have taught me." They lay in each other's arms until Mary noticed he had dropped off to sleep. She crept out of his bed, picked up her clothes and ran naked back to her room. She lay on her bed wondering what tomorrow would bring.

Lord Albert stirred and reached for his Irish rose but she was gone. Suddenly he felt lonely, sad and frightened. He didn't want her to ever leave him. She had brought so much laughter to this home, most unknown to her, but to those watching it was priceless. He could not comprehend that to have nothing and at aged nineteen to be wearing poor-girl bloomers, she had so much more to offer than a sophisticated English lady in all her fancy finery. It wasn't what a person wore, it was what was in their heart. He lay there waiting for the morning to arrive so he could see her again.

Mary wearily climbed out of her bed. Her morning sickness was still with her, but she couldn't let this be known. She would battle on. She had enjoyed last night and she knew she had pleased Lord Albert, as she saw the happy tears in his eyes. He was a kind man, but she was a little surprised to find he had a wooden leg. She wondered what had happened to him. She made her way down to breakfast only to find Lord Albert waiting for her. She smiled at him, letting him know she enjoyed last night. For this he was truly grateful, as he was worried she might think differently today, especially seeing his wooden leg. They chatted away about today's work. He would show her how to grow the seedlings, so when next growing season arrived they would have grown sufficiently to plant out into the gardens. Mary loved learning about new things. Her life had been very narrow and as she learnt more she began to blossom. Lovely colour had appeared on her cheeks, she had a healthy glow, but there was another matter that could also have been a contributing factor.

Tomorrow there would be a meeting of the gentry at Lord Albert's home. This was Saturday, Mary's day off. Tonight, as they dined, Lord Albert asked her if she would be available to help serve hors d'oeuvre to his guests. As always, she was only too willing to help. They went to the drawing room and talked about the meeting. Lord Albert looked at Mary tenderly and said to her, "Mary, please don't be afraid of me. I will never come to your room, but you are welcome in my room any time. Last night was very special to me. I would like to think it will happen again." Mary looked at him and smiled: "Indeed it will." Then she bid him goodnight. He sat there not believing what he had just heard. This Irish rose was full of surprises. Mary went back to her room and decided to open a drawer only to find it was full of beautiful undergarments. She had never seen such exquisite items. She lifted them out and spread them on her bed. There were silk and lace items, and they felt lovely. She put them against her bare skin and they felt so soft. Dare she try some on? The temptation was too great, so she chose the silk items, as they felt slippery and nice against her skin. She put on a silk bodice and some silk knickers; what a different feeling to her flannel bloomers. Mary stood in front of the mirror and combed her flaming red hair until it shone. In one of the drawers she found some jewellery, so picked out a red glass necklace and put it around her neck. She wondered if Lord Albert would think she was pretty. Mary decided to go and ask him. She quickly ran down the hallway to Lord Albert's wing. Just as she was about to knock at his door she saw the butler, who saw her and smiled. She knocked and waited until Lord Albert said to come in, then she opened the door and walked in. He was sitting in his chair by the window thinking about his Irish rose and here she was, his prayers had been answered. He had seen these items of clothing before on someone else, but never to reveal such beauty. Her hair fell loosely around her shoulders, silhouetting her breasts. The necklace was tucked under her hair and the red ruby was outclassed by his beautiful Irish rose. He asked her to come closer so he could look at her. "Do I look nice, Lord Albert?" she asked. His eyes filled with tears; such beauty, such warmth, so poor and insecure. He asked her to sit on his knee and he buried his face in her hair. His tears rolled down his face and were lost among her curls, but he could feel their dampness. He had never behaved like this before but he was completely powerless and overcome with this magical creature. She took his hand and led him to the bed, where she unbuttoned his shirt and took it off and ran her hands over his chest. She would let him do the rest, as he had to attend to his wooden leg. He asked if he could undress her and she stood as he untied her bodice and slipped her silk knickers off. Once in bed they caressed each other and he kept saying her name over and over again, pulling her into him until they became as one. He held her tight, never wanting her to leave, so he begged her to stay with him all night. Mary cradled him in her arms. This was where she felt safe. She needed to be loved, as starvation and poverty were again never far from her mind, especially now that she was with child. With this thought she drifted off to sleep.

When they stirred in the morning there was someone knocking on the bedroom door. "Come in," called Lord Albert. The door opened and in walked the butler, and he made his way to the window and opened the curtains. "Good morning, Lord Albert; good morning, miss," he said as he went about his duties. Mary ducked under the sheets to hide, but it was too late; she had been seen. Lord Albert laughed. "You don't have to hide, my Irish rose. Don't feel ashamed, you have made me so happy." And all the time the butler heard all this, as he was still in the room. Fancy Lord Albert saying those things about her when he was still in the room, she thought. He wasn't ashamed to be seen in bed with her; surely the butler knew what they did. With these thoughts she blushed and had a little giggle. Lord Albert loved it when she was happy. She still displayed such innocence; she was raw and natural, this was her world, the only one she knew. He never wanted her to be any different.

Today was the meeting of the gentry at Lord Albert's estate. Mary bathed and put on some lovely underwear she had taken from the drawers. She chose a beautiful dress. She was going to be serving the men that left her countrymen to die of starvation; she hoped she could keep her thoughts to herself, but she couldn't guarantee this. She brushed her flaming red hair until it shone like gold so they would know she was Irish. Mary wanted to look nice for Lord Albert, she wanted him to be proud of her. The meeting was held in the boardroom, then the men would move into the drawing room where they would be served drinks and hors d'oeuvre. She was nervous as she waited for the men to come through, but the butler was serving with her, so she wasn't alone.

After a few hours the men started to emerge from the boardroom and make their way to the drawing room where Mary and the butler stood waiting to serve them. They were loud and pompous until they saw Mary, then a silence fell over the room. Where had Albert found this beautiful Irish wench? He had not mentioned this to them so it came as a shock. No English gentry hired Irish servants; they bred like rabbits in poverty-ridden Ireland. But he had certainly picked a beauty — her hair looked like it had been spun from gold, and her cheeks flushed like a red rose. They would have to find out more about this beautiful creature.

Meanwhile talk resumed about the importing of their wheat from Ireland to England, as the Irish wharf workers had gone on strike refusing to handle any wheat that was to cross the Irish Sea. This was in defence of them being left to starve during the potato famine; these thoughts had never left them, as many lost family members to starvation. "The bloody Irish, they are trash, the famine was God's way of ridding them," said one pompous member of the gentry. Mary could listen no longer to their wicked talk and just at that moment Lord Albert came to Mary and apologised and asked her to leave the room. As she was leaving, one of the gentry grabbed her hair and called her an Irish wench. This was too much for Mary. She stood her ground and told her story. "My mother died aged forty-two leaving behind seven children. She died of starvation, she went without food to feed her children. How many of you pompous English gentry would do this?" "But you bred like rabbits," someone called. "In Ireland, poverty was everywhere. The only pleasures the Irish had was to lay together in each other's arms and make love, to forget what was unfolding around them. Why should they be denied such pleasures? You English have cold hearts and blue blood; Irish people have warm hearts and red blood," and with this, Mary fled the room. A silence fell over the gentry; this Irish lass had certainly told them what she thought of them. They had never given a thought as to why the Irish had such large families and how bad poverty was in Ireland. This had put a different light on the meeting, and the conversation switched to Mary. "Where did you find her, Albert?" someone asked. He told them the whole story, and that she was the best and most honest worker he had ever employed. "Do you bed her, Albert? I bet she is a fiery piece in bed!" someone else yelled out. Lord Albert told them all: "I have never met a more caring and loving person as my Irish rose. I would give up everything I own to have her by my side. No upper-class English lady could hold a candle to my Mary," he told them. This left the meeting in turmoil. Fancy giving everything up for a woman; this was unheard of by the gentry ... especially an Irish lass.

As they walked out to their carriages, someone called out to the men to come and see what was happening in the garden. There was Mary with a rose in her hair, her arms outstretched, dancing among the roses dreaming of her young Irishman, trying to forget what had unfolded in the drawing room. Her hair was flying in all directions, her dress was swaying with her movements, she floated round the rose beds like a magical creature from a fairy-tale. The gentry stood lost in this magical scene; how beautiful was this Irish lass. Now they understood Albert's plight. How they wished they had this unfolding in their back yards, more than that, how they wished they could be the one bedding her. They would never forget this scene, it was embedded in their minds; how they envied Albert. Someone clapped and this brought Mary out of her dream. She was so embarrassed, she ran off.

Lord Albert was upset with what had unfolded in the drawing room so he went in search of Mary to apologise. He had to find her; he had put her in a bad situation. He was angry with his fellow countrymen and angrier with himself. What if she had left him, what if he never saw her again? His heart was broken. He called the butler and the cook to help him look for her. The butler went to her room and knocked on the door but there was no reply, so he reported back to Lord Albert. "Sir, she isn't there." His Mary had stood up for her rights, what a brave lass, one to be admired. They searched till nightfall but still no Mary. He asked the butler to go back to her room and if she didn't answer, he was to go in. This he did, but still no Mary. Lord Albert was beside himself. He asked the butler to put a chair outside her door for him and he would sit and wait for her. At midnight the butler checked on Lord Albert; he was still there so he brought a blanket and covered him.

The next morning, he was still in his chair outside Mary's door. The butler had never seen him so upset and worried for him. He brought him some breakfast but he refused to eat, he had to find his Mary. With this he got up and went outside to continue searching. He just remembered he had not locked his garden storeroom so he went to check to see nothing had been stolen. As he opened the door, there lying on a sack on the ground was his Irish rose. She was curled up in a ball, her cheeks were tear-stained and her hair lay unruly on the ground. He wanted to lie with her and take her in his arms to protect her from the outside evils. He bent down then dropped onto his good leg and crawled beside her, enclosing her in his arms. If this tiny sack bed was all they owned, it would be enough for him as long as Mary lay with him. It all came flooding back to him what Mary had told the gentry about the Irish, that their only happiness was in each other's arms making love, taking their minds away from the poverty that surrounded them. He understood this now; here he was lying on a sack, but this didn't matter, all was forgotten, he had Mary. How he loved this lass. He felt tired as he had not slept all night. He drifted off to sleep with his arms around her, there on the ground in the garden storeroom.

Meanwhile the butler was still busy searching for Mary when he spied the garden storeroom door ajar, and he hurried over hoping to find her in there. He could not believe what unfolded in front of him: there lying on the ground was Lord Albert with Mary in his arms. They were both sound asleep. He stood and cried for his master as he watched them curled up together. How he must love her. He made his way back to the mansion to tell the cook to search no more.

Four months had passed since Mary had come to the mansion. The gardens were looking beautiful, they were her pride and joy. Even some of the gentry were coming more regularly to visit Lord Albert in the hope of seeing his beautiful Irish rose. She was the topic of conversation among the gentry and they had not forgotten what she had told them that day. But uppermost on their minds was the thought of Albert bedding her. What a lucky beggar; how they wished they too could have an Irish rose. But the English society would not like this. It was all right for Albert, as he had a more powerful title than them. They were just gentry — he was a lord.

Lord Albert was a bit sad, as Mary had stopped coming to his room. Had he done something to hurt her, did she not like him any more? He would have to ask. The next morning, she was late for work so he sent the butler to see if she was all right and as he knocked on the door, he could hear Mary crying in pain so he went in only to find her lying on the floor half dressed. He ran to fetch Lord Albert to come, who was quickly followed by the cook. "Mary, my lovely, what is wrong?" he asked. "The baby, something is wrong with the baby!" Why was she saying 'the baby'? What did she mean? With this the cook told him to go and fetch the doctor immediately. In a flash he was in the carriage on his way to get the doctor to his beloved Mary. It still hadn't sunk in: a baby, was she with child, his child?

It wasn't long before the doctor was attending Mary. She hadn't lost the baby, but she was on total bed-rest for the next month. He told Mary he thought she was just over three months with child, that was the danger period. When the doctor left, Lord Albert sat on her bed and brushed her hair away from her face. "Why didn't you tell me, my lovely?" he asked. "I was frightened to tell you I was with child in case you sent me away." "Oh, my Irish beauty, other than you this is my dearest wish, to father a child of my own." On hearing this Mary burst into tears. How was she going to tell him he wasn't the child's father, that the doctor had made a mistake as she was four months with child, not three. She asked to be left on her own as she was tired. Lord Albert bent down and kissed her. "This is the best gift you could have given me. I hope our child has your flaming-red hair. I will come back just before lunch to see how you are." He smiled at her as he shut the door behind him.

Mary was beside herself. If she told him the truth she would be an outcast, only to have to return to a life of poverty. She didn't want to bring a child into the same environment that she had suffered through. She couldn't go home as there were enough mouths to feed in that household, and she would not be able to support her family any more. Would it be so wrong for her to let Lord Albert think this was his child? If he knew no different he would love it as his own. The child would have a good life, she could have more babies with him so no-one would ever know, and she would be happy. She didn't feel the excitement when making love with Lord Albert. The passion was not there, not anywhere near like making love with the young Irishman, but that was the blue blood of the English versus the red blood of the Irish. But Mary knew she could live with this. She was never going to meet her young Irishman ever again, but she would not let that night slip her mind; it was a memory she could never forget, it was special ... now she had a reminder! She knew she was loved dearly by Lord Albert; she was his Irish rose.

She had made her decision. When he knocked on her door, she asked him to come in. He was so happy, he came and sat beside her on the bed and lifted her hair away from her face so he could tell her how much he loved her. The word love had never been mentioned simply because he didn't want to frighten her off, or for her to feel she had to make a commitment. He just wanted to leave everything open, but his biggest fear was that she would leave him. He lay beside her and nestled his cheek against her hair. "I was sad, Mary, that you hadn't been to visit me. I didn't think you liked me any more, but now I know. Why didn't you tell me?" Mary just smiled and put his hand on her swelling belly. Now he knew that it wasn't his fault that he and his ex-wife couldn't have children. This gave him great heart. While Mary was bedridden, he asked the cook to bring their supper to her room each night so they could dine together. He was so proud.

When Mary was able to leave her bed, Lord Albert wanted to take her into the city to buy some clothes suitable for her while she was with child. They shopped at the best stores, as he wanted her to look special; she had blossomed while with child. Mary asked if she could stop at a shop, as she had to do something. She went in and asked to speak to the manager. She still had the ticket she had taken off the stolen dress. She was shown into the manager's office and asked to sit down. She explained what she had done. "I know it was dishonest of me but I was desperate. Please tell me how much I owe you after all this time?" He was totally surprised that she had come back to pay, so all he asked for was the amount on the ticket. Mary thanked him for being so understanding and shook his hand as she left his office.

Lord Albert asked Mary if he could take her for a special supper to celebrate their wonderful news. While they were dining, a classy English lady accompanied by a younger man passed by their table, then she hesitated and came back. "Why hello, Albert, and who do we have here?" she enquired while looking at Mary. "Elizabeth, meet Mary. Mary and I are celebrating, we are expecting our first child." "Pleased to meet you," said Mary. "What do you mean, Albert? You can't have children," she told him. "Well, it seems I can after all," he answered with total delight in his voice. With this she scurried off. Mary suddenly felt sick; she found it hard to breathe and asked Lord Albert if she could be excused, then ran outside. She took a deep breath to try to regain her thoughts. Who was that? she wondered. How did she know Lord Albert couldn't have children? She was certainly upper-class English, and she knew him, as she called him Albert, but why did she mention about children? Mary went back inside and sat down. "Who was that lady?" she asked. "That was my ex-wife," he answered, then explained everything to her. Mary felt sad, as she was living a lie. Should she tell him the truth? But the thought of poverty for her child was too great, so she decided to bury the truth.

Another few months had passed and Mary's belly had swelled. The winter was just about over and she couldn't wait for the baby to be born. There were only three weeks to go by the doctor's reckoning, but Mary knew different. Things had changed in the mansion. Lord Albert had now become Albert and a nursery had been set up next to Mary's bedroom. It was furnished with all that was imaginable, as Albert was so excited about becoming a father. Mary tried to tell him they didn't need all he had bought for the baby, and that all that was needed was love, but because he was wealthy their thinking was different. Another week had passed and she was still with child. Mary knew the baby should arrive any day but she was hoping it would hold on for at least another week or two, as it would make it look a lot better. She got her wish and one week before the doctor's due date, Mary went into labour. Albert was on his way to fetch the doctor hoping she would not have the baby before they arrived back. She was in labour for six hours before she gave birth to a baby girl. The midwife wrapped the baby in a blanket and gave her to Albert to hold while she attended Mary. He looked down at his baby girl and loved her from that very moment. Once Mary was all finished the midwife took the baby and placed her by Mary's breast for her to start sucking. It didn't take long before she learnt where to go to be fed. Albert watched on in amazement; he was so proud. No way would his Irish rose ever leave him now. They were parents to this wonderful creation of nature. Now they had to choose a name. Albert knew from the moment he set eyes on his baby that her name couldn't be anything other than Rose. She would be his English rose.

She had her mother's red hair, but of course she would, she was totally of Irish stock.

3

Mary's Life Takes a New Twist

A year had slipped by and baby Rose was starting to crawl everywhere. Mary was visiting Albert again at nights and this cemented his love for her. He had asked Mary to marry him but she thought it was too soon, she wanted to wait. While baby Rose was sleeping, she would tend to the gardens, as she had grown to treasure growing plants from seeds then watching them grow into adults, as she called them. Albert still held meetings for the English gentry at their home. They now all treated Mary with respect; they could see the great joy she had brought to Albert's life. Many were jealous, as this Irish rose was definitely warmer than any English rose. They would often see her in the grounds with her wild red hair blowing unruly around her face, and she always shared a wave and smile with them.

As time passed, Albert begged her to become his wife; then he knew she was his totally. Mary relented and they were married quietly at the estate with no fuss. She didn't want her family to see the luxury life she lived, or know that Albert was a lord, especially her father. She was now Mary Rothchild, but she would keep it a secret for the time being.

One day a letter arrived to say her father was ill and he had asked to see Mary and her baby before anything happened to him. Her sister Norah had met a nice Irish lad and they had been married for fifteen months, so this would be a chance for her to meet him. Albert couldn't come but he insisted that Mary take baby Rose to meet her family. They had not seen each other since she left to go to London, which was coming up two years ago. Her family were happy she had met a wealthy man and that he looked after her well. They couldn't understand why she wouldn't marry him; perhaps if she had another baby she would change her mind.

Mary was on the train to Cornwall with baby Rose, and it was going to be a full day for them. They were going to stay with Norah and her husband in their lodgings, as Daniel, Margaret, Patrick and Julia were still all home with their father. They were grateful that Mary had been able to send money to help them, as their father was no longer working. The dust from the mine had affected his lungs, so his breathing was causing him great distress. But to keep their rented home, Daniel had now taken his father's job at the mine. Norah was at the station to meet Mary and baby Rose. They hugged each other, then Norah took Rose from Mary and cuddled her. She told Mary that she and Connor had been trying for a baby but it hadn't happened thus far. Mary knew how important it was for Norah, being Irish, to want a baby. They caught a carriage to Norah's lodgings, which was in a poorer part of town, when suddenly all Mary's past came flooding back. She shuddered to think this was her life; sometimes there wasn't enough money for food for the table, but the hardest thing for Mary was to know her mother had gone without to feed her family. Then to die of starvation, this broke her heart and brought tears to her eyes. In the two years since she had left, nothing much had changed; this was still the poorer part of England. She was grateful she was able to send money home to make life a little easier for her family. As they arrived, Connor was getting ready to go to work so Mary was able to meet him.

Norah called to Connor to come and meet Mary. When he walked in, there stood the young Irishman Mary had left behind in London. The one who had shared the bathroom, then her bed in the London lodgings, the father of baby Rose! They both recognised each other immediately, so to hide their embarrassment Mary went to him and gave him a cuddle telling him she was pleased to meet him. She stood for a moment looking at him; he was just as she dreamed, he was the one in her arms as she danced among the roses on the estate. He couldn't hide his excitement. "So, this is your Mary, what beautiful hair, and who do we have here?" he asked as he picked up little Rose. He held her high in the air, then cuddled her and held her close to his heart. "What a beautiful little girl," he said as he smothered her with kisses. Mary's heart was racing. Here was a father embracing not a stranger but his own little girl, not for one moment realising the truth as it stood before him. "I have to go. I will see you tomorrow,

Mary," he said as he made for the door. Norah kissed him goodbye.

They had lots of news to catch up on so after supper they sat and talked for hours. Norah could not believe how beautiful and happy Mary looked; she was the perfect advocate for life in the country, a privileged life at that. Her clothes were beautiful and little Rose was like a little doll. Her trip to London had certainly paid off, and Norah was happy for Mary. Her own life had not fared so well, as she became the mother figure for the remaining family when Kate left for overseas. It wasn't until she had met Connor that a little happiness came into her life. "How did you met Connor?" asked Mary; she just had to know. Norah had gone on a blind date; her friend's boyfriend had a friend coming down from London to work so they arranged for her to be his blind date. "When I saw him, Mary, I fell in love. I wanted him to be mine. He took a while to come around as he had been hurt by someone, and he still loved her." Upon hearing this, Mary's heart missed a beat; she wanted to run away where no-one would find her and cry her heart out. He had missed her as she had him. Mary had not told her family all the truths about her life. They had no idea her husband was an English lord and that he owned an estate. All they knew was he worked on an estate and was quite well off. She couldn't bring herself to let them know she lived the life of the English gentry because of the hurt they had inflicted upon the Irish.

But behind all this there was something that Mary didn't know. As mentioned, Albert was the largest absentee landowner in Ireland. His farms grew the wheat that was brought back to England during the famine. He had sanctioned for this to happen. This had to be kept from Mary. It wasn't until he heard her plight that he had even thought of the people of Ireland. They meant nothing to the English; it was just an impoverished country to them. But how things had changed. His mind was swinging towards Mary's people; just listening to her stories brought tears to his eyes. If not for the Irish, he wouldn't have his Irish rose.

"I will be gone in the morning when you get up, I have to leave for work early, so you go and spend the day with the family," Norah told her. With this they hugged each other goodnight. Mary couldn't wait to be on her own. She bent over and kissed her daughter — her and Connor's. She lay in bed feeling totally numb. Her sister's husband was the father of her child, but this he did not know or would ever know, but what a burden for her to have to carry for the rest of her life. Once Norah gave him children he would be happy. She lay there thinking of the wonderful morning they had at the London lodgings. She had never forgotten him or his passion; he was hungry for love, his warmth still surrounded her every time she recalled that unforgettable day. At some ungodly hour she dropped off to sleep. When she woke in the morning someone was sitting on her bed staring at her. She sat up quickly to find it was Connor. "Please leave, don't let Norah know you are here," she whispered. "Norah has gone to work. I waited for you, Mary, but you never came back. I went to your room but your belongings had gone. I cried each night waiting for you, you promised me you would come back. I worried that something had happened to you. I have thought of you every day since." He reached out and took her in his arms. On hearing these words Mary's heart was broken; she had missed him too. "Please let us keep our promise to each other," he whispered in her ear. This ignited the passion that had sat dormant for nearly two years; it was their first meeting all over again. They both got into bed and clawed at each other, pulling their bodies together feeling the hot passion in their veins, the Irish passion. Then Mary could feel that Connor was ready to take her so she yielded, pleading to him to take all of her. This she had dreamt of many times, and it was as beautiful as she remembered. He told her over and over how he had missed her and at nights he would cry out for her. This reduced Mary to tears. She couldn't bear to let go of him, so they made love again until they heard a cry coming from little Rose. "What a beautiful child, Mary, you are so lucky. One day I would love to have a little daughter like Rose," he said tearfully. The tears streamed down Mary's face. If only she could tell him that they both made this beautiful child together.

After pulling herself together, Mary made her way to the family home, pushing Rose in her pram. She had recovered enough to be able to face her father and her siblings. When she knocked at the door they all came running. "Look at you, Mary, you look lovely," they all commented together. Then her father managed to push his way through to see his daughter. Tears streamed down his cheeks. "My darling Mary, how beautiful you are," and he cradled her in his arms. He looked down and saw little Rose, so Mary picked her up and gave her to him to hold. He looked at her and told her she was his English rose. Mary had to drive back her tears; if only they knew that she was a full-blooded Irish rose. She couldn't get over how her siblings had grown. Daniel and Margaret were working to help keep Patrick and Julia at school. Daniel was working in the tin mine so they could keep their home and Margaret had a housekeeping job which she hated, but there weren't many choices for either of these siblings. Kate had emigrated to New Zealand hoping to get a nanny position on a sheep farm. No-one had heard from her as yet but letters could take months from the other side of the world to reach England. The family asked Mary many questions and she had to be careful how she answered them as she didn't want to expose her wealth to them. She told them about Albert and that he loved her dearly and was good to her. "Your mother would be so proud of you, Mary," her father told her. She noticed he was getting very frail so she asked him, "Is there anything I can do for you, father?" "Mary, I would love to go back across the Irish Sea to my homeland. I am not English and never will be. In fact, when something happens to me, I want to be buried near my home town of Ballydehob. Put your mother's ashes in with me, so we will be together again. It was work that brought me here, but Ireland is calling me home." Mary had saved some money and Albert told her to use some of their money for her family. Before she left she would see to it that her father got his wish to go home; God knows he deserved it for all the hardships he had suffered while bringing up his family. There were many stories told between them and the siblings loved having Mary visit them for a couple of days.

It was time to make her way back to Norah's lodgings as she would be home from work, and Connor would be at work. She kissed everyone goodbye until they met again tomorrow. Mary stopped off at a little store to pick up some supper and a bottle wine for her and Norah. She had to prepare herself to be able to face her sister; perhaps the wine would help. Mary fed little Rose and put her down as she had had a big day and was tired and grizzly. Then she took the top off the bottle of wine and poured them a glass. "You know, Mary, I can't remember when I last had a wine, this is lovely," Norah said. They sat and ate their supper. Norah was very much like their mother; she looked like she was carrying the weight of the world on her shoulders and it was hard to get a smile out of her. Sadly, she looked older than she actually was. Mary felt sad for her so decided before she left she would leave her nice clothes with Norah so she could look pretty for Connor. How she envied Norah to be lying in his arms every night, making love with him, but sadly this was not what was happening in her life. She told Mary that she and Connor were starting to drift apart, as there were no signs of a baby and this was upsetting them. "You know, Mary, we both desperately want a child but nothing is happening, so we have been advised to abstain from sex for a month so I can relax, and then it might happen." "Oh, that is so sad but it will happen, I know it will," said a confident Mary, as she was the one who would know — little Rose was living proof. They had a nice night together, as Norah had opened her heart to Mary. They would see each other the next day after Norah finished work.

Again, Mary lay in her bed and thought about her life. If she had a life with Connor it would be hot and steamy resulting in many mouths to feed. Could they have afforded to feed them? This would have been a big worry for them both. It was time for her to go to sleep as the dreams lingered on. When she woke she was not alone in her bed. There were arms surrounding her, and a hot body was pressing into her. Mary could feel Connor's manly parts ready to take her, and before she knew what was happening he had lifted up her nightdress and was on top of her, then he entered her. They both squealed in delight as they romped around in the bed. "Mary, I have never felt such pleasure since our first night," he whispered in her ear. "But you have Norah. She is a lovely girl, please make her happy Connor, she deserves it." "I know she is a nice girl, Mary, but she doesn't have your passion, she has no excitement in her body." This Mary had guessed, as she never looked really happy. "Promise me, Connor, you will look after her, I ask this of you?" she pleaded. "I'm sorry, Mary, I will not make promises that I don't know if I can keep. We made a promise to each other, it took a long time but we kept it, because I always believed our paths would cross again." This was enough for Mary to beg Connor to take her just one more time, as Norah would be home the next morning. They held each other and cried tears of sadness. This was the end for them.

Mary had decided to take all her family out for supper tonight. The only person missing would be Connor, but for Mary this was a blessing otherwise she might not have been able to hide her feelings. She would set the pram up so when little Rose was tired she could be tucked down for a sleep. Norah was coming around to the family home as soon as she came home from work, then they would all go out together. This was a special treat for them as this was something they could never afford to do. Mary spent a nice afternoon with her father. He reminisced about Ireland, and said he would never have crossed the Irish Sea to England if it wasn't for the potato famine. He still had siblings alive and he would love to see them before they passed away. Mary took enough money out of her pocket for her father to buy a return ticket to Ireland and spare money for food and lodgings. "Mary, I can't take this from you," he protested. "Father, this is in payment for a life of love you have given me. Please take it and visit your beloved Ireland. It will make me happy to know that you will go. You must promise me you will do this for me?" "Yes, I promise, Mary, I promise," he said.

School had finished for the day and Patrick and Julia had arrived home. They sat and asked Mary about her life in the country and told her they would love to come and visit her one day. She told them that she would love that, knowing it was never likely to happen. Mary never wanted her father to know she was married to an English lord. She felt sad about deceiving her family, but now wasn't the right time for them to know.

They all had a wonderful night out. Mary told them to order whatever they wanted, and to this family it was like Christmas had arrived early. She noticed that Norah was very quiet, but then she wasn't a person who let her feelings be known. This was not going to help her relationship with Connor as he was an outgoing person, and quite a handsome young man with the cutest dimple nestled in his chin. He had a charm that captured hearts, and Mary could see trouble brewing for Norah if she didn't show her emotions, as he was certainly a hot-blooded Irish lad ... as she had experienced! Norah spent a lot of time cuddling and playing with little Rose; she would make a wonderful mother, thought Mary. She prayed this would happen soon for them. They all walked home together and said their goodnights at the gate of the family home, then Mary, little Rose and Norah carried on to her lodgings. Mary put Rose to bed and went and sat with Norah. "What is wrong, Norah?" she asked. "Connor has been distant to me lately, Mary, I don't know why," she sobbed. "It will be all right, you are both stressed. Once you start bedding again it will all work out. Norah, I want to leave you some of my dresses. Put them on and look nice for Connor." "You always look so lovely, Mary," she said. She took Norah in her arms and cuddled her trying to reassure her that all would be fine. If only she could be sure.

This was the last night with her family as Mary was catching the train back to the estate the next morning. Because little Rose had had big days and was tired and grizzly, they all decided to come to Norah's so Rose could be put down to bed. Everyone was there including Connor, as it was the weekend. Mary told the family she had given money to their father to go back to Ireland for a visit, and asked them to make sure it was all arranged for him. She wanted it organised this week before it was too late. Daniel said he would book it on Monday and their father would be in Ireland by the end of the week. James's eyes shone, reflecting his tears of joy; he was at last going back to his beloved Ireland. "Don't forget, my children, that you are of Irish heritage, be proud of this forever. You were all born in Ireland, but sadly we had to leave it behind. I blame this on the English gentry who left our people to starve. Never ever forget your homeland, and who you really are ... We are Irish!

After hearing this, Mary burst into tears and ran to her father and hugged him. She was probably the one child most like him in her thinking of how badly the Irish were treated. She felt guilty of the life she had chosen and prayed to God that no-one knew her hidden secret. She heard Rose whimpering so went to attend her. She lifted her out of her bed and turned around; there stood Connor. "Please, Connor, go to Norah, she needs you, she feels neglected. Make me one promise, please love her?" He looked at Mary and asked to hold Rose. She gave her to him; he had every right to hold her and love her. "She is so perfect, Mary, her father must be proud of her." "Yes, her father loves her," she answered ... Oh how true! She took Rose from Connor and put her back into bed. As Mary turned around there was Norah standing watching Connor. "You two stay and talk to little Rose," Mary said as she walked out. Perhaps baby time might help them?

4

Life Back on the Estate

Mary was nearly home. The train trip seemed to take forever and little Rose was restless. Albert would be at the station to meet them and take them home. Mary had time to reflect on her trip back to visit her family, what secrets it had revealed, what emotions it had stirred within her. But most of all it brought back memories of her past, some she could never forget, others she was happy to leave behind. As promised she had left everything she wasn't wearing behind for Norah, hoping she would make an effort for Connor. She had even left her pretty nightdresses, hoping they might entice him to her, little realising the memories he was going to have when he saw Norah in them. She was going to miss Connor; between them there was a fiery passion that cemented a love that could never be equalled.

If she hadn't met him again, would her love have dwindled until it was forgotten? Was there an answer to this?

She was hoping she could still bed Albert and feel a little something in their relationship, as he loved her dearly, and provided well for her and little Rose. As soon as the train pulled into the station Albert spotted Mary's red hair through the carriage window. How he had missed her and little Rose; they were his whole life, especially Mary, who brought such joy to his heart. If nothing else, to feel her soft Irish hair brushing his face was enough to bring him the greatest love. He never forgot the first time her hair brushed his cheek in London when he was consoling her after her attack. That was where it all began. As Mary alighted from the train with Rose in her arms, Albert was right there to help her down and take Rose from her. "Oh Mary, how I have missed you. Part of my heart left with you, now I have it back. Thank God you are both home, my Irish rose and my English rose," he said as he kissed his daughter. This was enough to set Mary off and tears streamed down her face. She was confused, her mind was all over the place; who really did this little girl belong to? She was the only one who knew the truth, but two men owned her equally. It was a burden she had chosen to carry on her own.

It was good to be home on the estate. Mary missed the gardens and the luxury of the privileged life she had, although she never forgot her roots. This had been endorsed by her father; he would never let them forget they were Irish through and through and that their lives began in the little village of Ballydehob, County Cork, Ireland.

That night she went to Albert's room as she felt it was her duty to do so, as he had missed her. She would have been quite happy to go to her own room and relive those unforgettable moments with Connor, but now that was history once again. Albert sat and stroked her beautiful hair as she had let it out and brushed it for him. He felt it brushing against his face as he lay down beside her. Oh how he missed her. He took her in his arms, pulling her close to him, feeling her body connecting with his as he bedded her, muttering all the time how he had missed his beautiful Irish rose. She snuggled into Albert telling him she felt safe in his arms. But there was no excitement, no passion; she knew that she needed him, rather than loved him.

Six weeks had passed and Mary was right into her gardening. Her seedlings had grown and were ready to plant out into the gardens. Little Rose was now walking so Mary took her outdoors with her, as she loved playing on the grass. Today she felt sick in the stomach as she bent down to do the planting so she called it a day, as she thought it was just a tummy bug. But it persisted for the next week, then she realised she had once again missed her monthly cycle. This could only mean one thing: she was with child again. She was happy as now she knew Albert was the father; he would be thrilled. Mary decided to wait a couple of weeks before she told him. She did not go to Albert's room for the next week, hoping the sickness would pass.

Another month had passed and the gardens around the estate had never looked so picturesque. Albert loved that Mary cared so much for the grounds. He had another gentry meeting on Friday. This was to discuss the farming of the wheat crops in Ireland for the following season. They were all absentee owners but Albert was by far the largest landowner. His profit was way more than that of the other gentry. At the meeting they were going to take a vote on how much to increase the land tariffs to the Irish tenant farmers, thus meaning the farmers would get less income, but the gentry were getting increases for the price of their wheat. Where was the justice in this? Because Alfred had heard the plight of the Irish from Mary and how they had suffered, he was going to vote against this. He didn't want to cause the Irish any more pain. Mary had still not told Albert she was with child. She had been going to his bedroom regularly but tonight was the night to tell him. She would make it a special night for him; she would let him bed her and while lying in his arms she would tell him he was going to be a father again.

She went to his room with her hair falling down around her shoulders and wearing a lovely silk nightdress. Albert couldn't get over how beautiful she looked, she seemed to be blossoming with each day. He asked her to come and sit on his knee so he could brush her hair, as to him it was like spun gold. She couldn't have been more Irish and he loved her for this. "Come, Albert, I want you to bed me, I want to make you happy tonight," she told him lovingly. She went to his bed and waited for him to lay beside her. She caressed his body, working her hands down to his manly parts, fondling them until she knew he was ready to bed her. She slid her body on top of his but Albert couldn't wait he was so excited. He rolled her over pulling her close to him by her buttocks so he could take her. Mary let out a squeal of delight; this Albert had never heard before. How he loved this girl, she always surprised him. They lay exhausted in each other's arms. "Albert, I have a surprise for you," said a very smug Mary. "You always surprise me, my lovely." "But this is special. You are going to be a father again." Albert couldn't believe what Mary was telling him.

He sat up in bed and when he saw the tears in her eyes he knew. He lay down with her and cried alongside her. "My lovely Mary, you have given me more than I could have ever asked for in life. Please always be with me?" he asked of her.

It was Friday and the gentry were arriving in their flash carriages to attend the meeting. Mary and the butler were the hosts for the after-meeting hors d'oeuvre and drinks in the drawing room. Albert had asked her to let her hair hang loose around her shoulders and wear a lovely dress, as he wanted to try to persuade some of the gentry to vote against raising the tariffs. He asked Mary to stand with him and greet the men as they entered the boardroom. She had never been asked to do this before so was a little puzzled, but of course Albert couldn't tell her why he needed her to be with him. This had become a huge worry for him as Mary didn't know yet of his land holdings in Ireland. The gentry thought Mary was beautiful and intelligent, and Albert was a lucky man to have such a beauty. Their ideas of the Irish had changed a little since she had come into Albert's life, because of what she told them at their first meeting, stressing the plight of the Irish. Once the men had gone into the boardroom, Albert kissed Mary and thanked her. She left to attend to the food in the drawing room.

The meeting went on longer than usual and there were loud voices coming from the boardroom. As Mary walked past she heard someone saying, "You are outnumbered, Albert, the vote has gone in favour of raising the tariffs." Mary didn't understand what tariffs they were talking about, but she would ask Albert later. The gentry filed through to the drawing room for their usual after-meeting drinks. They all tried hard to win Mary's attention, as she was a great drawcard for the men. They wondered because she was so beautiful, would Albert be able to keep her happy? This was the talk among the men. They would be willing to step in and offer to help him out, it would have been a real pleasure. But this would never happen under Albert's watchful eye. Mary noticed that he was not his bright self. Had something gone wrong at the meeting? she wondered. She did hear that he was outvoted on something, perhaps it was important. With this, little Rose appeared and wondered among the gentry. "She is definitely her mother's daughter," someone remarked, as her red hair was like Mary's. "Yes, she looks Irish like her mother, for that I am very proud. I hope our next baby will be a replica of her mother also," said Albert in an authoritative voice. The men looked at him. "You lucky beggar," and they congratulated them both.

After they had all left, Albert went back to the boardroom and sat with his head in his hands, as he was upset. He had been overturned on the land tariffs review. If Mary heard the gentry were raising the rent for the Irish tenant farmers, she would think even worse of them than she did now. He was frightened he would lose her, as she had never forgotten the English for what they had done. This was where Mary found Albert, and when she asked him what had happened, he told her not to worry. "You have enough to worry about now you are with child. I will not burden you with my business, it really is nothing."

The months had passed quickly and now Mary had gone into labour. It was early in the morning so Alfred took the carriage to fetch the doctor and the midwife. When they returned she was in the last stages and in extreme pain. She panicked as she thought something was wrong, but as she battled on the baby arrived safely. They now had a son;

Alfred was beside himself, he was so proud of his Irish rose. The midwife took the baby away to let Mary sleep as she was exhausted. She hadn't seen her little boy but that would happen later. Albert cradled him in his arms and took him through to little Rose's bed to let her see her new brother. She leaned over and kissed him. What beautiful children I have, he thought, thus filling his eyes with tears. He didn't think he could ever have children and now he had two. How many more was Mary going to give him? The Irish were known for their large families, and Albert understood why — it was because they were warm and giving of love. The doctor waited until Mary stirred, he wanted to make sure there were no complications. The midwife fetched the baby and put him to Mary's breasts to feed. She was still drowsy as she held the little one and when she felt him sucking she closed her eyes.

When she woke, Albert was by her side holding her hand. The doctor had told him Mary had had a hard labour and she would be weak for a couple of days. He had brushed her hair and bathed her face, to him she still looked beautiful. She hadn't asked to hold the baby because she kept drifting off to sleep. Later in the day when Mary felt better, Albert propped her up in her bed and she asked him if she could see their little boy. He went and fetched him and lay him in Mary's arms. She looked at his little face and couldn't believe what she saw. There was the trademark dimple in the chin, the dimple that belonged to Connor. Albert watched as the tears streamed down her cheeks. She looked so happy, were these tears of joy … or tears of shock?

Mary cuddled him and fed him, then she wanted to go back to sleep. Albert kissed her and took the baby away. Mary was beside herself. This couldn't be, this was

Albert's baby, it had to be. But as she worked out the dates, yes, it could be possible. There was absolutely no doubt; the proof was right there staring her in the face. Then the sad realisation hit Mary hard: her two children were fathered by Connor, she had not conceived with Albert. Perhaps his ex-wife was right!

Mary had not told her family she was with child as she didn't want to upset Norah as she and Connor had still not conceived. One day a letter arrived from Norah. She sounded depressed as nothing had happened and Connor was drifting away. There was one piece in the letter that hit Mary to the very core of her heart. It read: 'The other night when I went into the bedroom, Connor was lying on the bed weeping into the nightdress you gave me, Mary, that is how desperate he wants a baby.' Mary read this over and over and she knew why Connor was weeping but thank god Norah didn't. He couldn't get over Mary, he loved her, she knew his heart ached for her. She felt sick, for she had not only betrayed Albert, she had betrayed her sister. She sat down and wrote a letter to Norah asking her to come and visit her. She asked Norah to get time off work and she would send money to her to get the train tickets. It would probably take a week for the letter to reach her.

Three days had passed and Mary was busy with little Rose and the new baby when she saw a uniformed man walking to her door. She thought it looked like a policeman, but why would he be coming to her home? "Does Mary Nyhan live here?" he asked. "Yes, I'm Mary." "I have some sad news for you. Can I come in? You may want to sit down." Mary invited him in. "Do you have a sister called Norah?" he asked. "Yes, is she all right?" "I'm sorry to have to tell you this but she took her own life last night. Her husband, Connor, found her this morning when he came home from work. He asked that you get the message as soon as possible. I'm very sorry," he said. Mary was heartbroken; she burst out crying. "Are you all right, is your husband here?" he asked. Mary said he would be home soon as he was at a meeting, but the butler was here. She just needed time on her own. She thanked the policeman and showed him to the door. Then she went back inside and sat down in a chair and sobbed her heart out. Little Rose came up and wanted to sit on her knee to give her a cuddle as she could see her mother's tears. Mary tried to be brave in front of her little girl, as she looked as if she was going to cry with her. Poor Norah, the stress must have been too much for her to bear. She wondered how her father was going to take this; it would break his heart. She would have to go to him as soon as possible, as early as tomorrow. Then she thought of Connor. What a terrible thing for him to have on his conscience; were things really that bad between them?

5

Heartache Hits Mary's Family

Mary was on the train back to Cornwall. Albert wanted her to be with her family at this sad time. He would keep Rose with him but Mary would have to take the baby as she was still breastfeeding him. They hadn't talked about a name, as she had yet to fully recover from giving birth. She would catch a carriage from the station to the family home, then worry about where to stay. She was still reeling from Norah's death. The carriage stopped outside the family home and Mary climbed down with her baby. No-one knew she had given birth. She knocked on the door and it was opened by her father. He couldn't believe this was his Mary, as no-one knew she was coming. Tears streamed down his face as he embraced her. "Tell me, father, what happened to our Norah?" she asked. "She had been sad for a long time, then she had just found out she was barren and that was the end, she didn't want to live any more." Then he noticed a little bundle tucked into Mary's breast. "You didn't tell us about this little one?" "How could I, father, when I knew how desperate Norah was for a baby. I couldn't let her know I was with child; how unfair would that have been?" she said sadly. "You are so considerate, Mary, you are the sensible one of the family." This made her feel so guilty; if only he knew of all the people she had betrayed.

"Father, is Connor at home?" asked Mary. "Yes, he is making the arrangements for Norah's funeral. Perhaps you should go and see him, he will need all the support he can get." "Are you sure you are okay by yourself?" Her father assured Mary he was okay, as Patrick and Julia would be home soon. With this she kissed him and left to walk to Connor's lodgings. She knocked on the door and waited until Connor opened it. When he saw Mary, he went to rush into her arms. "Be careful, Connor, I have a passenger," and she pointed to the baby. "I'm so sorry, Connor, why did she do this? Things couldn't have been that bad, could they? Did you do as I asked, did you love her?" "I tried, Mary, but it is you I love. Norah could never be you. She was a sad person and when the doctor told her she could never be with child, her world ended. It wasn't easy for either of us but we did try, I promise you that," he sobbed.

Suddenly there was a little cry so Mary undid the wrap from around her neck that held the baby. She lifted him out and cuddled him. Connor looked at him and asked if he could have a cuddle so she put the baby in his arms. He looked at him and immediately noticed the dimple. His brain went into overtime: did this coincide with Mary's last visit, was this his child? There was the trademark dimple, one that had come down through Connor's family with each generation. He held him close to his heart, smothering him with kisses. It was then he realised the truth, that this was his and Mary's son. "Mary, this is our son, I know because of the dimple. Why didn't you tell me?" he asked. "Connor, this is so complicated, no-one must ever know, this has to be our secret. I didn't know until he was born whose son he was, whether he was yours or Albert's, but the minute I saw the dimple I knew. Albert thinks he is his son and that is the way it must stay," said a teary-eyed Mary. "But I want to love him too, Mary, I have a right, he is my son, our son," he begged. Poor Mary, this was just too much for her, as she was still trying to get well. She broke down and had a howling session not knowing what to think any more. Her world was collapsing. Connor cradled her in his arms; this is where he wanted to be, with his Mary. For the past two years he had harboured a broken heart. How much longer could he carry on? "Connor, please let me get well again and breastfeed our baby, then I will think about things. It is too much at the moment, I can't handle any more pressure. I have to be well to breastfeed. Promise me you will give me time to sort things out?" He could see that Mary was under terrible pressure and it was affecting her. "Yes, Mary, I will give you time, it is unfair of me. I must grieve for Norah." With this he kissed his son and gave him back to Mary. They said their goodbyes until tomorrow when the whole family would come together for Norah's funeral. She walked back to be with her father and siblings. They were all home when she arrived. It was a sombre household, everyone remembering their Norah, as she was the first of their siblings to leave them. Mary went into the bedroom to feed her baby. Julia had arranged to sleep on the settee and let Mary have her bed in Margaret's room.

Mary asked her father to tell her all about his visit to his homeland. "Mary, it is my home. I want to end up back in or near Ballydehob where it all began, where I met your mother, where we made our family. Promise me you will take me back?" he pleaded. "If that's your wish, father, then that's what will happen. Did you catch up with all your brothers and sisters?" she asked. Her father told her he had a wonderful time. Things were still tough and there was still poverty but the Irish were resilient and were starting to bounce back, but it would take a long time. "You know, Mary, I received a letter from my brother yesterday and he told me the bloody English gentry have decided to raise the land tariffs for the Irish tenant farmers. Once again, the Irish suffer at the hands of the English. That is why I will not be buried on English soil." Then the conversation she had overheard at the board meeting back at the estate all came flooding back. Is that why Albert was so upset? He mustn't have wanted the land tariffs to be raised, that was why he was outvoted. But why would Albert be involved in the voting? Surely it was only the absentee landowners who had voting rights? Obviously, he had stood up for the Irish. Was this because of her?

It was the day of Norah's funeral. Everyone walked around to Connor's lodgings. As he opened the door, Mary saw that he was sad, his eyes red and swollen. She just wanted to take him in her arms and cuddle and love him, but today was about Norah. They had arranged for two carriages to take them to the church where Norah's body lay. The priest knew her well as she had been doing a lot of praying lately, asking for the child that she could never have. He spoke kindly of her. Mary stood up and spoke of the conversations they had together, remembering that all the time she could never have what she wanted most, it was not to be. "We don't have you, Norah, but we will always have wonderful memories. You are at peace now, goodbye, dear sister." Connor was genuinely heartbroken. He had tried to love her, but in the end, they were lost from each other. She was only ever second to Mary right from the start, but he had told Norah when they met he was still trying to heal from a broken heart. She had accepted him on those terms. His heart had been broken that night back at the London lodgings when he waited for Mary but she never came back. That dream had never left him and when he saw her again, it all began where it had left off. And now he had a son that he was going to lose to someone else, his life was a mess. He sat and cried for Norah, Mary and his son, he was losing them all. He could see no end to any of this! After the service they went to the burial to be with Norah while she was put in her final resting place. Their father cried, as he didn't want to leave his beloved daughter; they had to take his arm and lead him away. Mary had her baby strapped to her breast; thank God she had his warmth to get her through all this. They all went to the family home for a cup of tea. Mary tried to stay away from Connor; she was afraid her feelings would be picked up by other family members.

Meanwhile Connor sat consumed with self-grief. He never wanted to lose Norah this way; she was a caring person. In the end it was never going to work between them, but he did not foresee this happening, she was too young. His eyes turned to Mary. She was so vibrant, so beautiful and she had their son strapped to her breast. He wanted to hold them both but that would have to wait. He told himself this was Norah's day. The next morning Mary took a carriage to the train station. Only her father knew she was leaving. She couldn't face Connor; he only had to say the right words to her and it would start all over again. She needed time to get well and work things out. Her little baby had been so good; all he did was sleep.

Six months had passed and Mary was healthy again. Baby Joseph was growing fast and little Rose loved him, she was always bestowing kisses upon him. Mary had been visiting Albert again at night but he was mindful of what she had been through with the last birth so he had refrained from bedding her completely. He would just lie in her arms and let her hair brush his cheeks; this was enough at the moment, as he didn't want her to be with child again. It seemed she was very fertile, so he would give her time to enjoy the children. One night while lying in his arms she mentioned to Albert what her father had told her about the English gentry raising the land tariffs to the Irish tenant farmers. This was hurting the Irish again. Were they not happy leaving them to starve during the famine? Why could they not be respectful to them, and allow them to get back on their feet? "There always has been and probably always will be that rift between the two countries," he said. "But Albert, why do the rich gentry own so much of the Irish land? It doesn't seem fair to me." "Mary, my lovely, years ago the King of England, who was a Protestant as were most English people, took the lands from the Irish and gave it to his knights and people who supported him. This was to suppress the Irish, as they were known to 'breed like rabbits'. He could see that the Irish Catholics were multiplying at an alarming rate, so he planted Protestants among them encouraging them to marry Irish people so as to take the lands from them. The Protestants and the Catholics have been at loggerheads for many years. I don't know if it will ever change. We of the gentry were brought up to dislike Catholics, it was born and bred in us. Most of the gentry families only had one or two children, thus being the accepted thing. But the Irish had large families; it was thought that was why Ireland was poverty stricken, so many mouths to feed. England never suffered on the same scale. But, my Irish rose, there is nothing we can do to change things," Albert told her. "Who votes on the raising of the land tariffs, is it only the gentry who own land there?" Mary asked. This was getting too close to home for Albert, and he wanted this conversation to end right here. "You know, Mary, your father is old, all he remembers is poverty, but things are changing in Ireland," Albert told her. He held her in his arms and hoped to God she never found out about his holdings. If so, he would definitely lose her, this was a certainty!

Joseph was now one year old. Mary had thought of Connor many times. The family had mentioned in letters that he had gone back to Ireland, and this made her feel sad as he was missing out on seeing his son grow up. Mary knew he would be hurting but he promised to give her time to think things over. One day as she was playing with the children in the garden, she saw a strange carriage pull up. It stopped for a couple of minutes then it headed away, which she thought was strange. The butler must have attended to it, perhaps it was someone for Albert, but he was at a meeting in town. She continued playing with Rose; Joseph was crawling around trying to join in, he was so funny always trying to out crawl himself until he tipped over, then he would get frustrated. "Look, Mummy, someone is there," said Rose. Mary looked up and there stood Connor, still as handsome as ever but a little more grown-up looking. She ran into his arms; not a word was spoken, it didn't need to be, their body language said it all. He let Mary go and ran and picked up his son. "Hi, young man." He held on to him and smothered him with kisses, whispering to him telling him how he had missed him. Rose was watching this strange man cuddling her brother. Who was he? "Hello, young lady, how are you?" he asked. Mary couldn't take her eyes off Connor; the passion and love was still there in her heart. It was as if he had never left her. "Where have you been all this time?" Mary asked. "Once again you left me, Mary, without a word. You broke my heart again. I went back to Ireland to let you sort yourself out, but I couldn't wait any longer, I had to see my son. This last year has been a life sentence for me. I have shed so many tears wondering what he looked like; how I have missed you both so much. Is this where you live? God, Mary, it is beautiful, I can understand why you came back here, look at the gardens, how wonderful for the children. You look just as I always dreamt, you are still the most beautiful lady I have ever set eyes on, the one I fell in love with in the London lodgings. What are we going to do, Mary? I can't walk away from my son." Mary didn't know what to do, she knew this day would come, but she had always put it to the back of her mind hoping it would just go away ... but here it was!

Connor sat and played with Joseph and Rose, making them laugh as he rolled on the grass; he was just like a big kid. This is what Mary loved about him: nothing was impossible, he was just an ordinary guy enjoying himself. Albert was not a hands-on man. He was a looker, not a doer; it would not be proper for him to roll on the grass. What was she going to tell Albert? He would be home soon. "Connor, what if I tell Albert that you are my cousin and have come to stay, until I work out what we are going to do? But you must promise there will be no showing of affection between us. You can play with your children each day." As soon as she realised what she had said, Connor had caught on. "What do you mean, Mary, my children?" "Rose is your daughter. I was with child when I met Albert, but he didn't know, so I bedded him as soon as I missed my monthly cycle. I didn't even know your name, I couldn't contact you, we were total strangers who knew nothing about each other." Mary explained how she met Albert, about her gardening position and what happened from there. "He is Albert Rothchild, he is a nice man and has been good to me. He loves me, Connor, how can I tell him the truth? It would break his heart. He pleads with me never to leave him. He was married but they couldn't have children, now he has two, who he thinks are his own. I can't tell him otherwise, imagine how he would feel. I am bedding him to see if he can give me a child of his own. I have missed my monthly cycle so am praying I am with his child. Perhaps you could get a job around here, that way you could spend time with the children. Would you do this for me?" she pleaded. "We can't bed each other as we know we are both fertile. I must give Albert a child. It will be hard for us both but God knows we have waited this long." "How do you think I feel about you bedding Albert? I hate the thought, Mary," he replied. "Please, Connor, if you love me you will wait."

"Daddy, Daddy," called Rose. With that Albert had returned and was walking towards them. "Connor, please?" whispered Mary. Rose ran to Albert and he picked her up and cuddled her. "Hi, Albert, we have a guest, this is my cousin Connor, he will be staying with us," said Mary. "Pleased to meet you, Connor," acknowledged Albert. "What a beautiful estate you have here," Connor replied. "Yes, this was my family's estate, it passed to me when my father, Lord Charles Rothchild, passed away." For goodness' sake, he must be a lord, thought Connor. No-one had told him this, that was because none of Mary's family knew. She had kept it a secret. "Come, let us have a celebratory drink," said Mary as she picked up Joseph and kissed him. They walked towards the mansion. Connor could not believe his eyes, such luxury. How could he expect Mary to give all this up? What could he offer her other than love? But he was the father of her two children, that was deserving enough for him to be with Mary. He didn't have the slightest inkling Rose was his daughter. Mary had given him two beautiful children. As they entered the hallway the butler took Albert's coat and hat and hung them on the coat rack. "Please prepare a room for Mr Connor, he will be staying with us," Albert told him. "Yes, sir," he replied. With that they entered the drawing room and Rose went and sat on Albert's knee while Mary handed Joseph to Connor while she poured them a drink. "I can see where Joseph's dimple comes from, it must be a family trait?" said Albert. "Yes, it seems to turn up in the male line, but we can lay claim to it," said Connor proudly. Albert excused himself to tell the cook there would be an extra guest for a few days. Connor looked across at Mary. She was beautiful, just like everything that surrounded her. All he could see was wealth, but was Mary really happy? Albert seemed a nice man, but he lacked a warmth that should be surrounding Mary. She deserved it. I would give her all the love in the world, but would it compensate for all the privileges that came with Albert? Connor wondered.

They dined together with the children. Rose was

warming to Connor and went and sat on his knee. He ached to kiss and cuddle her but he had to restrain himself; this was not the time or the place to let his feelings be seen. Albert excused himself and went to his office as he had work to attend to. Mary and Connor played with the children and such laughter had never before echoed so loudly through the home. Although Albert loved the children, he didn't play with them as such. He liked them sitting on his knee or holding their hands but physical play didn't take place. Connor asked where her and Albert's bedroom was. When he learnt that Albert slept in one wing and Mary slept in a separate wing, he couldn't believe it. Who would not want Mary in their bed every possible moment to hold her and love her? This was not a life, this was upper-class pompous gentleman type behaviour. Irish people didn't live like this, they knew the enjoyment of having someone lying beside them, someone to share their love with. This meant if Mary wanted to be bedded she had to go to his room. How so upper-class was that? thought Connor. This really annoyed him; this was servant-like treatment.

He would ask Mary when he had her on her own how she felt about this; he was disgusted. She was busy getting the children ready for bed. "Give Uncle Connor a kiss," she told them. "Where do the children sleep, Mary?" he asked her. "They sleep in my wing next to my room." That meant Albert didn't help attend to them through the night. He retired to his wing and saw them the next morning at breakfast. How bloody English is that? he thought. Connor started to see a lot of flaws in Mary's life. It all looked glamourous from the outside but within lay a certain sadness. How could this be a fulfilling life? It was not! "Oh Mary, what a wasted life, what wasted love, my darling, you deserve more. I could give you so much more," he whispered to himself.

Once the children were down, Mary came back and they sat and talked. They had to be careful what they said, as Albert or the butler could appear at any time. Mary told Connor about the gardens and how she propagated the plants from seedlings, then transferred them into the gardens and watched them grow into adults, as she called them. Mary and the children spent a lot of time outside while Albert spent most of his time in his office. Connor asked Mary what Albert did. Mary couldn't tell him as she didn't really know, but he held meetings with the gentry in his boardroom, and he attended meetings elsewhere. She said he never discussed business with her. So, she wasn't even included in his business interests, how sad was that? Connor could see so many negatives unfolding in Mary's life. This might be how the English gentry lived, but it was not a life as such for someone of Irish descent. Tomorrow he would ask her if she was happy with her life!

The next morning the household was busy as the children were being attended to by Mary. Connor asked if he could help so she gave him Joseph to dress. He bounced him on his knee making him laugh, while Albert sat and watched on. Is this what happens every morning? wondered Connor. Mary had been to visit Albert last night as he was back bedding her. This had been happening for over two months now, and Mary was sure she was with child, but she would not tell him yet. As she looked at Albert she could see he wasn't well, so told him to go back to bed. "Yes, I think I will, my lovely, come and see me soon," he said. With that he headed to his room. Once the children were fed she asked Connor if he would take them for a walk. She put Joseph in the pram and away they went. He was happy to help Mary with the children; it gave her a break, and him time with his family.

Mary went to Albert's room only to find the butler attending to his good leg. She got a terrible shock to see his toes were black and swollen; she hadn't noticed them when she visited him at night. Then she remembered the last few times when she visited him he was already in bed, so she would not have noticed them. "Albert, what is wrong?" "My diabetes has attacked me again, I didn't want you to see this. Now I have to go to hospital and have my other leg amputated," he said. "Is that why you already have a wooden leg? Why didn't you tell me?" "I didn't want you to know in case I lost you, my Irish rose," he sobbed. "Oh Albert, you have been so good to me and our children, I would never leave you," cried Mary. "Come here, my lovely," he asked of her, and they lay together on the bed, her hair brushing his cheeks.

Albert went to hospital and had his leg amputated but his recovery was slow, as complications had set in. Before he went in he asked Connor if he would stay on at the estate and look after Mary and his children, seeing he was family. This suited Connor as it gave him time to bond with his children. He took them for walks around the estate and played games on the lawns with them. He cared for them while Mary visited Albert in hospital. Albert would not let Mary see his amputation; he was frightened if she saw it he would lose her. She would sit with him and he would stroke her beautiful hair, which brought him comfort. Unbeknown to Mary, Albert had called his lawyer and made out his will; with it was a letter which was to be given to Mary upon his death. It was to explain his land in Ireland, why he had hidden it from her, once it was hers it would be her decision as to what she wanted to do with it. He knew her hatred for the absentee English gentry landowners, he had tried to help, but he was outvoted, he couldn't go against his countrymen, but she could.

Mary had never thought of life without Albert, but things had become complicated with Connor now on the scene. Mary's heart was torn. Who had the right to the children? She totally loved Connor, but she cared deeply for Albert because he had rescued her from a life of poverty and starvation. She dreamed of sharing a bed with Connor each night, falling sleep in his arms and waking up to find she was still in them in the mornings. The English gentry life was totally different to that of the Irish. They liked to have their own space and their own bedroom, it was a superior thing with them. Connor had not had time to ask Mary if she was happy with her life, if she was happy with the bedding arrangements, and if she felt less of a being, by what he considered as outcast treatment of her. He thought it was a division of class, not fully understanding how the wealthy lived and how they were bought up. They were the superior beings ... they were gentry and lords!

Tonight, when Mary came home from the hospital, Connor wanted to know where he stood with her. She had refused to show any affection towards him and he found this hard to cope with. Of course, the butler and the cook were always around; this Mary was well aware of. She didn't want anything to get back to Albert, not while he was so sick. They all had supper together; now Rose insisted that she always sat next to Connor as he was always joking with her and she loved the attention. Joseph was just starting to walk so Connor spent hours with him encouraging him to take off. Mary was grateful for him being here with the children as she was spending a lot of time at the hospital encouraging Albert to get better. Connor bathed Joseph and prepared him for bed while Mary tended to Rose. Once they were settled Mary poured her and Connor a drink and they returned to the drawing room. The butler had asked for the night off as he had business to attend to, so would be back before supper tomorrow night.

As they sat enjoying time-out together this was a chance for him to start asking questions. "Tell me truthfully, Mary, how do you feel about sleeping in your own quarters on your own without someone's arms around you, without the love of a man to keep you warm?" "It took me a long time to get used to. I thought when Albert took me as his wife it might have been different but it wasn't, but that is the way of the gentry. They are not Irish, Connor, not hot-blooded like you and me. They are of blue blood, there is a cool aloofness about them but it is their upbringing, they were brought up to believe they were superior. I know this, that is why Albert loves me. He calls me his Irish rose; he has never known such love before he met me. He said English roses were prim and selfish; he loves my unruly red Irish hair and my openness." "I know all these things about you, Mary, but all I want is to love you, for you to give me your pleasures, no-one else. I don't want to share you, please let me love you tonight, we are here on our own," he pleaded. "But Connor, Albert is lying in hospital so sick, how can I be happy?" she asked. "Just for one night, Mary, give me one night, please, one night?" he begged. Mary could not ignore Connor's pleas. Her heart melted, it was that Irish charm, that Irish warmth that flowed through his veins. She took his hand and led him to her room. They stood and looked into each other's eyes, then that fiery passion overtook them both. They grabbed at each other's clothes ripping them off while running their hands over each other's bodies touching the appropriate places building up a passion that only they knew. The flame was ignited and they hadn't made it to the bed yet, but there was no other feeling on earth that could match what was about to happen. There were squeals of delight as they fell onto the bed. Connor pulled Mary hard into him until he felt her hot body positioned ready for him; this was the finale, it was raw passion, that of which the Irish knew and loved. Mary lay crying in his arms, only in his arms did her emotions flow through her body and strike her heart like a bullet. He had unlocked her heart ... snapped the padlock! The passion did not stop there, it flared many times during the night. Mary was thankful she was with child as she had no worries whose baby she was carrying, and it wouldn't be long before she would not be able to be bedded. By morning she lay exhausted in bed. Connor told her to stay there; he would attend the children. This had never happened before as Albert was not a hands-on person. When he rose in the morning he expected all to be done. Connor was in boots and all; he shared the family duties because he loved his children. They were the reason for him to get up every morning to help dress them and start their day with a happy beginning. He left Mary to lie in as long as she liked, God knows she needed it, she'd had a busy night!

Connor was playing with the children on the lawn when Mary rose. She came to the door and watched this happy family ... her family. Before the butler arrived back, Mary wanted to talk to Connor so she asked him to come and sit with her. "Connor, last night I gave you myself completely. You are my dearest love, and I am asking you to be patient a little longer. Let me get Albert well again, I promise I will not bed him any more. Once he is better, and I have given him his child, I will make a decision. I have not told him yet I'm with child. I ask this of you." "My darling, after last night I will wait forever. I have my children, they will keep me happy, but you will always be with me in my heart."

The butler arrived back and everything was on track. Mary went to the hospital to spend time with Albert. He wasn't well today, he had a temperature so was in isolation. Mary was allowed in but she had to wear a mask and sterile hospital gown. She sat down beside him and he reached out and stroked her hair. She took hold of his hand and squeezed it, as he was a little delirious with a fever. The doctor told her not to come back for three days until the fever subsided so she went home with a heavy heart. It took three weeks for the fever to leave him. He was very weak and now had an infection in his leg. Mary was heartbroken, but she decided it was time to tell him she was with child. This time it was his very own child. Albert was thrilled; his family was growing, soon he would be home. Another three months went by and Albert was still not home. His amputation was causing concern as it was still not healing. When Mary visited him, she would lay his hand on her belly so he could feel the baby kicking, and this kept him happy. He didn't talk much as he was still very weak. The doctor asked Mary to come to his office and told her unless the wound healed he was in danger of more infections. Another six weeks passed and at last he was on the mend, and if he continued he could be going home in two weeks' time. This meant he would be home just before the baby was due. He would be in a wheelchair for at least six months before they could think about another wooden leg. Now Mary could bring the children in to see their father. Joseph was walking everywhere and Albert couldn't believe how he had grown, but it had been nearly nine months since he was admitted to hospital.

Mary was a little concerned about the baby's arrival, but she didn't have to wait long as that night she went into labour. The butler took the carriage to fetch the doctor and midwife while Connor waited with Mary. He bathed her face and told her he loved her; it broke his heart to see the pain she was in. When the doctor arrived, he told her it was going to be a long wait, that she had to be brave. Four hours had passed and Mary lay exhausted, but then a big pain and scream helped push the baby out. The doctor told her she had a little boy. The midwife cleaned him up and put him in Mary's arms. He was definitely Albert's son as he was totally different to the other children, but then he would be! For this she was grateful. Albert had proved he wasn't the reason his ex-wife could not have children, but only Mary knew this. She put him to her breast and he hungrily started sucking, there were no problems in this department. When Mary was ready to sleep the doctor brought the baby out to Connor to hold. He rocked him back and forth; he had never handled a newborn baby. He wished it was his baby, but Albert had been kind to Mary and he knew it would be Albert's only child, because Mary was never going to bed him again. He felt a warmth to this baby, as Mary was its mother. When she woke she walked out unsteady on her feet, and she loved that Connor was holding the baby. As she bent down and took the baby from him she whispered a 'thank you' to him, then headed back with the baby to her bed.

This morning the butler got the carriage ready to bring Lord Albert home. They had discussed that they would not tell him of the baby's birth, they would place him in his arms when he was settled in at home. Just before lunch the carriage pulled up and Rose ran to see her father. The butler lifted him out of the carriage and put him in his wheelchair. "What's wrong, Daddy?" she asked him. "It's all right, Rose, I will be better soon." He was wheeled into the drawing room where Mary came out with a little bundle and put it in his arms. "You have a son, Albert." "What do you mean, Mary, I have two sons," he said. Mary's eyes filled with tears. If only you knew, Albert, this is your only son. He held the baby and rocked him. "He has dark hair, Mary, where is the Irish hair?" he asked. "This little one takes after you, Albert, he is our English child. I want you to name him." Albert thought for a moment then he announced, "We will call him Charles Rothchild after my father Lord Charles Rothchild. Connor was sitting in on this and took it all in. So, what was this lord thing? He would ask Mary the significance of it at a later date.

Albert thanked Connor for looking after his family and now that he was back they could manage. But he is in a wheelchair, what could he do to help Mary with the children? thought Connor. "I think I will retire now, my Irish rose, come and see me in ten minutes," he said as the butler wheeled him to his room. Connor did not take kindly to Mary being summoned to his room. What about the children and the newborn baby? It was as if she was a servant; things were going to be different now that Albert was home, demands were going to be put on her, how would she manage?

Mary told Connor that Albert said he could get him a

job at a gentry's estate just a couple of miles away as he needed a handyman. "Please, Connor, take the job. You can come each Sunday and see the children. I will keep my promise to you, I will not bed Albert again. Please give me another six months as I have to breastfeed Charles and Alfred will get stronger. I can't leave until the baby can manage without me. He will have to stay with his father, he won't let me take him when I leave, but we have Rose and Joseph." "How can I leave my children, Mary? I love them," said Connor. "This will be the last time I ask you to wait for me, I promise," pleaded Mary. Connor told Mary he would do it this one last time, but after that, decisions would have to be made.

Another three months had passed, and Connor was working on the neighbour's estate. He came every Sunday for lunch and stayed for the day playing with the children out on the beautiful lawns, while Mary tended her beds of roses. She would wheel Albert out and he would sit for a short time, then asked to be taken inside to his office where he wanted her to sit with him while he stroked her hair. She could see Connor and the children playing and longed to be there with them. To throw caution to the wind, when she was in the garden working, all the time she was near Connor, they whispered precious words to each other. Baby Charles was growing but he was a grizzly baby, always wanting to be picked up, then the grizzling would stop. Albert couldn't bear his noise so was always asking Mary to pick him up and cuddle him to quieten him. This interfered with her time to spend with Rose and Joseph and this upset Mary. "Albert, I can't be picking him up every time he cries, he will expect this all the time, and will turn into a spoilt child," said an angry Mary. "I will take him to the nursery so you don't hear him. He has to have his crying sessions." "But Rose and Joseph didn't cry like Charles, is there something wrong with him?" asked Albert. Mary tried to explain that all children were different, that they had been lucky with the first two babies. Even when Mary put Charles on the floor to have a kick he cried. Albert was continually asking Mary to pick him up. One day when this happened she took Charles over to Albert to nurse and took the other children outside. She could hear Albert calling to her but she ignored him as she was angry. Let him see if he can quieten him, she thought. Ten minutes later she came back and Charles was asleep in Albert's arms. "See, Mary, he just needs to be cuddled." "But Albert, this can't happen each time he cries, if we start this he will rule us, this is not going to happen. You will just have to put up with a bit of noise," said an angry Mary. Never before had there been words between Albert and Mary but it was happening more often since Charles was born. Albert had changed since his operation; he was less patient with the family and had become more possessive towards Mary. As there were more children to care for, there was less time for Albert; this he didn't understand or like. He had been asking Mary why she wasn't coming to his room at night as he wanted to bed her. She told him she wasn't ready yet, but it would happen soon, knowing it was never going to happen. After her last night with Connor she could not give herself to Albert as there was no passion between them. She had given him a son, she could give him no more.

The six months was nearly up and Mary was dreading having to tell Albert that she was going to leave him, and to admit to her betrayal with Rose and Joseph, but he did have his own son in Charles. He was still waiting on his Irish rose to visit his room each night but she did not come. Just when he had given up, one night there was a knock on his door and in came Mary. She lay on the bed with Albert letting him rest his face against her hair, but she told him she would not bed him just yet as she didn't want another baby. He agreed; just to have her beside him was enough to make him happy. If he was happy with this arrangement she would visit him more often, as she wasn't breaking her promise to Connor. Albert at least deserved a little comfort at nights for the life he had afforded Mary. But how was she going to tell him when the time came?

6

Mary's Life Changes Forever

Mary had one week to tell Albert; she was heartbroken that all had to be revealed. She had been visiting him each night as he hadn't been feeling very well so she afforded him the pleasure of having her lie with him. Tomorrow night was the last night she would visit him, but it would be to tell him something he never wanted to hear from her. When she got out of bed this morning she was upset with herself for what lay ahead. While she was attending to the children she heard the butler calling her. "Miss Mary, come quickly, it's Mr Albert, something is wrong with him." She rushed down the hallway to his room and could see he had a terrible fever. "Don't go in, Miss Mary, you must fetch the doctor. I will stay here," he advised her. She ran and picked up Rose and Joseph, electing to leave Charles in his crib, put the children in the carriage and away they went to fetch the doctor. When they arrived back the doctor went straight to attend to Albert. He was only in his room for a few minutes when he came straight out and told Mary he had another infection; they would have to get him straight to the hospital. Between them, the doctor and the butler lifted Albert into the carriage. "Come and see me, my Irish rose," he called to Mary as they drove away. "I will, Albert, I will come." Her promise to Connor was going to be broken again. She would have to stay and nurse Albert until he was well again, she couldn't abandon him now. Was this her destiny, forever caring for Albert? What about Connor? How long would he wait, and the children, what would happen to them? Connor would never leave them, he would take them with him as they were his, he loved them. She couldn't deny him of them any longer ... where to from here?

Mary couldn't visit Albert as the children weren't allow to see him because he was in isolation with the infection. On Sunday when Connor came to visit, Mary had to ask him to look after the children as she had to visit Albert; she had promised him she would come. It had been three days since she had seen him. He cried when he saw her. "I thought you had left me, my lovely," he sobbed. "Oh Albert, I had no-one to look after the children, but Connor came today so he is with them." "Come and sit by me, my Irish rose, let your hair brush against my cheek, you are so beautiful. Please never leave me. When I come home, please come to my room, Mary, I want to bed you again." Mary had to turn away, she could not look at Albert. For her, life was getting more complicated with each day. How could she leave him now? But she knew one thing: she could never bed him again. The red-hot blood of the Irish had outweighed the cold blue blood of the English. If she couldn't bed Albert, then her duties at the estate were over. She would miss all the luxury but she was not happy any more. As she said her goodbyes to Albert, he asked her to come back tomorrow. "But I can't, Albert, I have the children to look after." "Ask Connor to look after them," he told Mary. She explained that he had a job, she couldn't expect him to take time off. "You must come, Mary," he insisted. This put more pressure on her, she felt trapped. She was in a terrible state when she arrived back at the estate. She climbed down from the carriage in tears and walked towards the home. Suddenly it all became a blur and she fell to the ground. The cook saw it happen and called for Mr Connor. He came racing out to see what had happened, only to find Mary lying on the ground. He called her name but she was totally out to it. He lifted her up and carried her into the drawing room, laying her on the settee. He asked the cook to wet a cloth so he could bathe her face. Rose and Joseph were crying seeing their mother lying there. "What is wrong with Mummy?" asked Rose. "She is very tired, she will be well soon," Connor told her and gave them both a hug. Charles was in his pram grizzling away but he was forgotten for the moment. As Connor bathed Mary's forehead, she slowly came around. "I can't cope any more, it is too much," she sobbed. "I will help you, Mary, you are not on your own. I will come back and look after the children so you can rest," he told her. He asked the butler to help him walk Mary to her room and they lay her on the bed where she dropped straight off to sleep. Mary wanted to close out the world, her brain was shutting down on her. Connor asked the butler to make up a room for him as he would stay and care for the children so Mary could visit Albert. He put the children in the carriage and drove to his place of work to ask for a week off explaining what had happened. They weren't happy about this so Connor told them he would finish. These Irish, who did they think they were? First, they had an Irish neighbour who went out of her way to snare Lord Albert and now this? He was a good worker, they had to give him that, but sadly he was Irish. The gentry weren't yet accepting of the Irish. Connor gathered up his belongings and drove back to the Rothchild estate with the children. The cook had supper ready so he fed the children and got them ready for bed. Charles was still grizzly so he took him into Mary as she was still breastfeeding him. She had just woken and was staring at the ceiling trying to work out what had happened. Connor propped her up in bed so she could feed Charles. He bent and kissed her and left her with the baby. He would talk to her later and find out what was wrong.

After everyone was settled including Charles, Mary bathed and changed and brushed her hair. She walked into the drawing room looking lovely and a little happier. "What happened today, Mary, that brought all this on?" asked Connor. "Albert cried when he saw me, he thought I had left him after not visiting him for three days, but he forgets I have the children to care for. He told me he wants to bed me when he comes home, but I can't go there. Then he insisted that I visit him tomorrow but I can't take the children, so what do I do with them? I don't know what to do, Connor. I can't even keep my promise to you, the six months has just passed, I can't seem to work anything out any more," she sobbed. "Mary, forget the promise to me, go and visit Albert tomorrow. I have finished next door so I will look after our children. Make up some milk and leave it with the cook and we will attend to Charles. He is not an easy baby to look after but we will manage." "Albert spoilt Charles; he insisted that I pick him up every time he cried. I argued with him about this, but he couldn't stand the noise, so I had to do as he asked, he wasn't well so it was peace at any cost ... this is the cost!" "Things will change while he is not here," Connor assured Mary. She smiled; how she loved this Irishman. It was time for Mary to go to bed as she was tired. Connor told her to lie in and he would see to the children in the morning; all she had to do was feed Charles. Mary thanked him; she couldn't wait until the time was right for them to be together.

The next morning Mary took the carriage to the hospital to visit Albert. She had to wear a sterile gown and a mask as his infection was worsening. When she saw him he looked so sick. He beckoned for her to come and sit next to him; they weren't allowed to have contact with each other. He smiled at her and closed his eyes as he knew his Irish rose was with him. Mary sat and drifted off herself; she came to when she heard Albert choking. She panicked and ran to fetch someone. When they came back into the room Albert was lying very still. The nurse ran to him to take his pulse but alas there was nothing, he had passed away. The nurse told Mary not to touch him, to leave the room until she fetched the doctor. She sat outside the door crying for Albert. When the doctor did eventually arrive and attend to Albert, he told Mary to go in and say her goodbyes but not to make contact with him as he was riddled with infection. He told her he would come to the estate tomorrow to talk to her. Mary left the hospital and drove the carriage home. Strangely she felt a peace come over her. Albert would suffer no more and the pressure had eased. She would miss him as he had taken her away from poverty and replaced it with abundance; in return she had given him four years of happiness and a son. She was his beautiful Irish rose.

It was lunch time when Mary arrived home, and Connor was surprised to see her home so early. He walked the children up to meet her, only to see her eyes were swollen and red, she had been crying. "What has happened, Mary?" he asked. She told the children to go to the nursery, she would be along in a minute as she had something to tell them. This just left her and Connor. "Albert was so pleased to see me, Connor, he told me I was his Irish rose, then he closed his eyes and drifted off to sleep, never to wake. He passed away with his Irish rose by his side," she told him through her tears. "Oh, Mary, I am so sorry, what are you going to tell the children?" he asked. She didn't know how she was going to tell them, but first she had to tell the butler, who would be so upset as he had been in the Rothchild household for many years, and also the cook. She asked them both to come to the drawing room; they could see she was upset. "I'm sorry to have to tell you this sad news. This morning Lord Albert peacefully passed away, I was by his side." This brought tears from both of Albert's loyal servants as this was the end of an era. Now Mary had to tell the children, but they were young. Rose was four, Joseph was two and Charles was still a baby. She told them their daddy had gone to heaven as he was sick and he would be looked after by the angels. Neither of them really understood, so questions in the future would come up from time to time about their daddy.

No-one had thought of the future. Mary knew nothing about the running of the estate, where the money came from. Albert had told her nothing; he was lord of the estate, this was his business. She didn't even know if she had a home or what would happen to the estate, she was completely in the dark. Tomorrow the doctor was coming, then she would have to make funeral arrangements. She didn't know how she was going to pay for it as Albert handled the money. She had no access to the estate money. Who would she go to, did the butler know anything about his affairs? Thankfully she had savings of her own, not a lot but enough to get by on for a couple of weeks. How did the butler and the cook get paid? She would leave this worry until tomorrow, she had had enough sadness for today. After the children were in bed, the cook, the butler, Connor and Mary all met in the drawing room and talked about Albert's life. Mary asked the butler if he knew anything about Albert's estate but he told her to go to his solicitor as Albert would have made a will explaining everything. Mary only knew the last four years of Albert's life, as she didn't like to ask questions of him. The butler told Mary about Lord Albert's father, Lord Charles Rothchild. He was a very wealthy man; his money and his lordship had passed down to Albert on the death of his elder brother who had died when he was eight years old. Had he lived he would have inherited the estate and the lordship. Now that Lord Albert was gone, the lordship would pass to his first-born son. "Does it have to go to the first-born son?" asked Mary. "Yes, that is what happens down through the English gentry," he replied. This was another problem that was facing Mary, as Joseph was not Albert's son. Charles would be entitled to the lordship, but on paper Joseph was Albert's first-born. Only Mary and Connor knew of this. On this note they all decided to call it a night, as sad as it was. Their master had gone.

Mary told Connor she would see him tomorrow. They both knew this was a delicate time, and Mary wanted to grieve for Albert. She lay on her bed and cried her heart out. She never thought about Albert leaving her, this was the last thing she expected.

The next morning the doctor came out and talked to Mary. He told her to arrange the funeral as soon as possible, especially with Albert's body being so infected. Mary cried when he told her this. "Be brave, Mary. Albert loved you dearly, he was very happy." With this he left. Mary drove the carriage into town to make the funeral arrangements. She explained how Albert had died so the funeral was arranged for the next day. This left no time for people to know but it had to be attended to. She went to Albert's church and spoke with the minister. She left all the arrangements to him, as being Irish and a Catholic she wasn't familiar with the Protestant religion. Because he knew Albert was a lord, he agreed to put it all together in a hurry. He told Mary it would be a big funeral as all the gentry would attend, and that they usually had a cup of tea and cakes at the estate of the deceased after the funeral, so this would be expected of her. Who was going to pay for all of this was Mary's immediate worry, but if it was the right thing to do, it must be done for Albert. She bought some flour and other ingredients so the cook could make some cakes and bread for tomorrow. It was all a bit of a rush but it had to be done because the doctor had told Mary it was important for Albert to be buried as soon as possible. Only Mary, the funeral people and the minister knew of this. Mary was so grateful for Connor, he was so understanding, so very helpful, but one day when she had finished mourning for Albert, she would reward him handsomely.

Today was Lord Albert's funeral. Both Mary and Connor dressed the children in their best clothes; Charles would have to be in his pram as he wasn't walking yet. The cook had been up all night making food for today, Mary had helped to make sandwiches and set up the formal dining room for the guests arriving after the funeral. It was a busy morning. At last she had a little time to get herself ready. She brushed out her hair, and put on Albert's favourite dress. As she stood before the mirror, there was the image of Albert's Irish rose with her unruly red hair. Tears welled up in her eyes as she reflected back on her life with Albert here on his estate. What was going to happen next, would they be homeless? But today was for Albert. The butler drove Mary, Connor and the children to the church. The cook stayed on at the estate to prepare the rest of the food and have the water boiling to make the tea when they started to arrive. There were carriages everywhere and many people were filling the church, Mary was amazed. As they made their way into the church, people looked at Mary. She was so beautiful and what a lovely family, they all looked very Irish of course with their red hair, all except the little one, he looked English. Connor held Charles so he wouldn't grizzle. They sat in the front pews of the church with Rose and Joseph looking around at all the people; they were too young to understand any of this. The minister who took the ceremony said kind words about Lord Albert, as he was a respected gentleman of the gentry. "Lord Albert was the largest absentee landowner in Ireland, his wheat exports to England were of vital importance during the potato famine, as this had kept England from suffering the same fate as Ireland." On hearing this, Mary went into total shock. No, this was not right, Albert was not part of that.

She stood up. "Are you sure that is right?" she asked. A deadly silence fell over the church. "Yes, Mary, Lord Albert saved the lives of many English people," said the minister. With this she couldn't contain herself. "At the expense of the Irish," and she sat down with tears streaming down her face. All the time she lived with Albert she had no idea he was one of those greedy English gentry that took the wheat out of Ireland, leaving them to starve. Was this what all those meetings in the boardroom were about? But she remembered hearing that he had been outvoted; had he tried to make amends because he loved her?

Several of the gentry stood and talked about Lord Albert, saying that he had never been so happy since finding his beautiful Irish rose. She had given him a family, made him happy and they were sorry he wouldn't be here to see his family grow into adults. He had been taken too soon. After the service had finished the minister came to Mary and shook her hand offering her his condolences. She thanked him for the service; she was going to apologise for her outburst, but she could not hide the bitterness she felt. Many of the gentry talked among themselves about Mary's outburst, none of them realising that Lord Albert had not mentioned to her about his Irish holdings.

The carriages all drove to the Rothchild estate for the expected cup of tea. Connor took the children away from the home after dropping Mary and the butler off; he didn't want her to have the worry of them. Everyone expressed their sadness on hearing of Albert's passing. Some of the gentry just couldn't help themselves. Albert had not been buried five minutes and already some of them were lining up for a piece of Albert's 'Irish rose'. She was such a beauty, shame to be wasted! Mary was approached by a lady whom she recognised as the one that talked to Albert the night they dined at the inn a few years back, in fact it was Albert's ex-wife. "Hello, Mary, we have met. I'm sorry to hear of Albert's passing. I owe you an apology, well, Albert really. I was the one who couldn't have children, it wasn't Albert; your youngest son is so like him. Congratulations." Mary was stuck for words. "Yes, Albert was happy to know he could father children," was all she could think of to say at that moment. Some of the gentry that came to the board meetings approached Mary. "What will happen to Albert's Irish lands? We need them as part of our bargaining power," they said. Mary told them that because she didn't know of these lands and what was happening, she could not make any decisions. The sly old dog, they thought to themselves, perhaps Mary was going to be a pushover for these randy gentry ... how very wrong they were!

A gentleman came up to Mary while at the estate and said he was Lord Albert's solicitor, could she come to his office tomorrow morning for the reading of his will? He told her where to come and to be there at eleven o'clock and they would go through it together. Mary thanked him. The cook had catered well as there was plenty of food for everyone. People were walking around the grounds admiring the flower beds and the roses. One of the gentry relayed the day of the board meeting when they came out to the gardens to see Mary dancing around with her arms outstretched and her red hair flying wildly in the breeze; it was likened to a fairy-tale. That was the day she gave them a lesson telling how the Irish had suffered.

When everyone had left and it was peaceful again, Connor returned with the children. They had a lovely afternoon — they had been to a stream where he let them paddle. They ran to their mother and told her what they had done. None of today's events had registered with the children, to them it was just a little different from a normal day. Mary sat down with the cook, the butler and Connor to reflect on the day; everything had gone well apart from Mary's outburst at the church. She asked the butler if he knew of Lord Albert's holding in Ireland. Of course he did, as he had been with the family for many years, he was Albert's private butler all that time. He now thought it was time for himself to retire; it was the end of an era. Lord Albert was gone and there was nothing really left here for him. "Miss Mary, I feel this is the right time for me to retire, so I will finish up at the end of the week. I hope you will forgive me?" he said. Mary explained she didn't know what was happening with the estate, whether any of them would be there, depending on what was in Albert's will. With this the butler smiled, as Lord Albert had discussed his will with him. Mary didn't mind; if she was staying they wouldn't need a butler, besides it was better for him not to see what was going to unfold on the estate, if indeed they were able to stay.

The next morning Mary was sitting in the solicitor's office anxious for the will to be read, as her future on the estate was uncertain. "Have you any idea what is in Lord Albert's will?" he asked Mary. She told him they had never discussed a will as he was still young. "Lord Albert was a very wealthy man. He owned the estate and was a large landowner in Ireland, in fact the largest absentee landowner. He has a very large sum of money in the bank, which along with all he owns is now yours and the children's. You will manage the estate until each child reaches the age of twenty-one. What you do with it up until that time is entirely in your hands. You own half the estate and the other half will be shared among Rose, Joseph and Charles. There is the question of the lordship. It goes to the first-born son; this does not include illegitimate children, but there is no worry there, as it will go to Joseph. Also Mary, Lord Albert left you a letter to read upon his death, he loved you dearly. You are a very fortunate lady, but beware of those who seek to take your fortune from you. If you have any questions, please ask me." Mary just sat; she couldn't believe that Albert had left her everything he owned, he must have loved her dearly. She had become a very wealthy and powerful lady. "What land did Albert own in Ireland?" Mary asked. "He owned land from County Cork to Dundalk. He had huge wheat farms." "Who farms them?" she asked. "Some are tenanted by Irish farmers, others by English farmers. The gentry tried to get all English farmers but of course not many English were eager to settle in Ireland or work for a mere pittance," said the solicitor. Mary thanked him. "I will be able to speak to you any time," he told her. "We will have to go to the bank and change the signatures before you can use the money. Do you want to do it now? We can go together." Mary agreed as she needed money to pay the butler, so off they went. The solicitor arranged all the legal documents that had to be signed, making Mary the owner of the Rothchild estate. She thanked him and he told her he would bring out any other documents that needed to be signed. Then he handed Mary the letter from Albert.

All the gentry were talking about Lord Albert's estate. Who would benefit from it? Surely it wasn't all going to be left to his 'Irish rose'. That would mean it would no longer belong to the English gentry; they didn't want any Irish intervention. He was the largest landowner and produced the bulk of the wheat crop. How would this affect them? If it was left to Mary there was likely to be a shake-up in line for the gentry. They would have to wait until the gossip surfaced on the contents of Lord Albert's will.

Mary drove the carriage home and found the children and Connor playing ball on the lawn. She asked them to come and sit down as she had something to tell them. Connor was worried as he had walked away from his job at the other estate. "You and your mummy own this whole estate and huge farms in Ireland. Daddy left us everything, we are rich," she told them. It all went over their heads as they were too young to understand, but Connor did. "What do you mean, Mary, can we stay here?" "Yes, my darling, it is all ours," she said. "But we must be respectful to Albert. The butler finishes next week so we will be very discreet for one month until everything settles down. Connor agreed as there was going to be plenty of talk around town without adding to it with a scandal. "Let's go in for supper," said a peckish Mary. They had a nice family supper together then played games until the children's bedtime. As Mary was relaxing she remembered Albert's letter to her. She asked Connor if she could be excused so she could read the letter in private. She would be back soon. Mary lay on her bed and opened the envelope and started to read:

My lovely Irish rose. I hope you don't have to read this letter for many years after it was written as I want to spend all of my life with you and our children. I have never known such happiness, such devotion and such beauty you have given to me for these years. There is one betrayal on my behalf, Mary, and that is my ownership of Irish lands. I couldn't tell you as I couldn't bear the thought of losing you. Until

I met you I never spared a thought to what the people of Ireland were going through, it must have been terrible to have grown up through the potato famine. It was you who changed me, that is why I voted against the raising of the land tariffs, but I was outvoted. Because I was part of the gentry I didn't have the guts to make changes but if you read this letter in time you can change things. Please remember to keep the estate running, you must have the income from the Irish lands, but how you run them is up to you. It might be time for you to look after your own people. I entrust my estate to you and our children. My title of Lord passes on to our first-born son, he becomes Lord Rothchild. Goodbye, my beautiful Irish rose. Forever, Albert.

At the beginning of Albert's letter Mary was sobbing; by the end she was wailing. What a beautiful letter, to think he had one betrayal. What if he had learned of her two betrayals? Would he have forgiven her? They had betrayed each other for different reasons, but to think he hoped she didn't have to read this letter for many years, broke her heart. It was only months ago that he had put pen to paper and written this. "Oh, Albert, I'm so sorry you have left us, but where was it all going to end? In total heartbreak, that of which you could not have handled, so I say goodbye, my darling, you have been spared," she whispered among her tears. She couldn't go back and face Connor, she had to deal with this first, in the silence of her own mind. She walked down the hallway into Albert's room and went in. Nothing had been touched since he left for hospital. She lay on his bed and cried her final tears; this was closure.

When Mary woke the next morning, she jumped out of bed to go and fetch Charles to feed him, but he was gone. She looked at the time and it was mid-morning, so she didn't panic as she knew what had happened. Connor would have got him up and fed him his bottle, so she could have a lie-in. She bathed and dressed then made her way to the dining room, and there were her family all being looked after by Connor. "Thank you for all this, Connor, I'm sorry I didn't come back last night. After reading Albert's letter I just had to grieve. I went to his room and lay on his bed and said my final goodbyes." "It's all right, Mary, you don't have to explain, I understand. You just buried your husband, of course you are going to want to mourn," replied Connor. He put jackets on Rose and Joseph as they were going to the woods to look for squirrels. "Do you want me to take Charles on my back?" he asked. "No, leave him here with me, I need some time with him on his own." She picked up Charles and hugged him. This was definitely Albert's son. He was not as loving as the other children; he definitely had the blue blood of the English running through his veins.

Then the thought of the title of 'Lord Rothchild'. Rightfully it belonged to Charles as he was Albert's first-born son, but to the outside world and by the birth papers this belonged to Joseph. She would have to talk to Connor about this; his son was Irish, he couldn't possibly take on the English title of 'Lord'. Mary didn't want her Joseph to become part of the English peerage. He was Irish through and through; not a drop of blue blood ran through his veins.

A month had passed and the butler was gone. The only staff left was the cook. Both Mary and Connor thought it best if she went too, so no gossip would leave the estate. Mary was sad to tell her they didn't require her services any more, but they had decided to run the estate on their own. She would leave them in two weeks' time. They also talked about Mary's family. Patrick had left school and was working in the tin mines with his brother, Daniel. Mary wanted better for her brothers as she had seen how the dust from the mines had affected her father's health. Mary decided to remove the English tenant farmers from her land and replace them with Irish farmers. This would be an opportunity for Daniel and Patrick to live a better life as tenant farmers back in their homeland of Ireland. Her father was still alive but his quality of life was poor; no-one thought he would have survived this long.

Today Mary was at the train station. Her whole family were arriving, as she and Connor had decided they needed to know some truths. But not all! Also, they would give the siblings the opportunity and a choice to become tenant farmers if they so wished. As the train pulled into the station they could see Mary's red hair. Margaret and Julia helped their frail father alight from the train while the boys tended to the luggage. There were hugs all round. Mary's family were in for a big shock as they had no idea that Albert had passed away and that she had been left the estate. She had so much to tell them, but the biggest shock of all would be to see Connor. They piled into the carriage; it was a tight squeeze but everyone was excited. At last they were going to see where Mary lived and meet her husband. As they drove through the countryside and saw the beautiful estates, their excitement grew. Never had they see such riches. When Mary approached her driveway, she pulled the horses to a stop. "Look at that beautiful estate. What do you think?" she asked everyone. They couldn't believe what stood before them. "Who does that belong to?" they asked. "Lord Rothchild did own it but he passed away a month ago. Now it belongs to his wife," she said. "Oh my God, imagine owning that," said

Margaret. "Let's go and visit her before we go home, would you like that?" asked Mary. "But Mary, we can't do that, we don't even know her," said Margaret. Mary gave the horses the sign to carry on up the driveway. The girls were fluffing around with their hair wanting to look nice to meet this important person. As they pulled up outside the entrance there standing in a line were Connor holding Charles, and Rose and Joseph. No-one moved, they were in shock. "What's Connor and your children doing here, Mary?" they asked. "Let me introduce myself: I am Mrs Rothchild and this is my estate." "No, Mary, this cannot be yours. Where is Albert?" asked Daniel.

After they had time to sit and talk, Mary explained her life that she had hidden from them, about Albert passing away, and now it was time for her to explain Connor's appearance; this was going to be the hardest part. Mary told them what had happened that night at her London lodgings, how she was meant to come back but her life took another twist, then how she ended up at the estate. She dreamed of meeting this handsome young Irishman again for many months, but her life with Albert had begun. "Little did I know I was with child; Rose is Connor's daughter. It wasn't until I came home and stayed with Norah that I met Connor again. A year after Norah passed away, Connor came to find me." The family were stunned to hear this from Mary; they had no idea that her life was so complicated, so exciting and so sordid, depending on who thought what! Mary's father burst into tears, this was too much for him; his beautiful daughter had a child to Norah's husband. She went to him and asked for his forgiveness, she knew he would be hurt. "I need to rest, Mary," he said. She took him to his room and helped him lay on the bed. "Please forgive me, father, my life has led me to tell lies, but my heart is in the right place." "I know, Mary, I know. I just need to take all this in," he said. She put a cover over him and left him to rest.

The rest of the family thought this was a thrilling story mixed with excitement, romance and sadness, but no-one hated Mary for what happened. They were very happy that Connor and Mary had found each other again. Mary explained that she was still mourning for Albert so they were not together yet. She had elected to leave out that Joseph was Connor's son, as this would open a can of worms that would deeply hurt her family, perhaps divide them! She told them to wander around the estate and enjoy themselves. Rose and Joseph told them to follow them and they would show them some squirrels. Connor thanked Mary for explaining everything and leaving sensitive issues untold. Together they prepared supper for everyone, as the cook had finished. They loved it just the two of them on the estate, but they had not bedded each other since Albert's death, as Connor would wait until all Mary's emotions for Albert had disappeared. That night when the children were settled in bed, Mary called a family meeting. Her father was seated in a comfortable chair, as there were more secrets to be revealed.

"Father, this is going to be a shock to you, but please bear with me until all is explained. I only found out at Albert's funeral that he was the largest absentee English landowner in Ireland. He was part of the gentry that brought the wheat back to England, leaving our people to starve. He couldn't tell me because he knew how much I hated the English for what they did, and he didn't want to lose me. If I had known I would not have been here today. He was Lord Albert Rothchild." "Oh my God, you married a lord?" asked Julia. "Yes, and the lordship passes to Albert's son." "This is so exciting," said the boys. "There is a silver lining to all this. I am going to replace the English tenant farmers with Irish farmers. No longer will they rule our lands. I am offering you, Daniel and Patrick, the chance to become tenant farmers in your homeland. I will place you both on your own farm and you will work for me. I have to keep the land as that is what supplies the income to keep this estate going." The brothers could not believe what was being offered to them — to leave the tin mines in Camborne for the life of a farmer back in Ireland was beyond their wildest dreams. "Father, you can go back to Ireland and live the rest of your days with the boys, they will care for you," said Mary. She watched her father's eyes light up. "I'm finally going home. Thank you, Mary. Thank you, my darling daughter." "Now we have Margaret and Julia. What would you like to do, my sisters?" asked Mary. Margaret said she had always dreamed of working on an estate. Could she come and cook and garden here with them until she got enough experience to apply for a position on another estate? "You both talk about it and let me know," she said. Julia was an academic and wanted to go on to have a higher education. "I will pay for you to have whatever education you want, Julia. You must do in life what is in your heart," Mary told her. Julia thanked Mary, as she was going to have to leave school and get a housekeeping job that she would have hated. She cried with happiness and hugged her sister. The home they lived in in Cornwall belonged to the company that owned the mine as it was only rented, but when the boys left for Ireland, Julia would have to find lodgings. This Mary would sort for her. "My darling Mary, you have made your family very happy and very proud. We all thank you from the bottom of our hearts. For this good fortune to come to our family, we must thank the Lord," said her father, and with this he said a prayer of thanks.

The following morning there was such excitement on the estate. Everyone knew what their future held; Mary's good fortune had cemented a future for them all. She told the boys she knew very little about the Irish lands, that she and Connor would go to Ireland and sort things out. Now that Margaret was coming to work for them, she would look after the children for a few days while they made the trip. The boys' lives would carry on as usual at the tin mine until the Irish lands were all sorted, as it meant they still had a home.

Mary was sad to see her family leave but she had brought them such joy; all she had endured had paid off. Margaret was returning to pack her belongings and to give notice to her employer, then returning as soon as possible. This was her dream come true, due to the good fortune of being Mary's sister. It would never have happened for her otherwise, as to get a position on an estate one had to have previous experience, so now she was on her way! As Mary was driving home from the station she had to stop her carriage as there was something blocking the road. She noticed two men standing on the road in front of their carriage, and they asked her to climb down as they wanted to speak to her, but Mary refused to leave her carriage. "What can I do for you gentleman?" She thought she recognised them from Albert's board meetings. "What are your intentions for your Irish lands? Albert was our mainstay, we relied on his knowledge and his support. We hope you will continue along the same lines?" they asked. "I can assure you I am going to make changes, but I will not discuss business here. You can call a meeting and come to my boardroom," said Mary. "We of the English gentry don't allow women at our meetings, we are a gentlemen's club," was their response. "Please yourself, gentlemen, if you wish to know my intentions call a meeting in my boardroom. Now may I pass?" "You must be lonely without Albert. You are too beautiful not to have someone to keep you happy," said one of the gentry. "I am Irish, you gentlemen are cold-blooded Englishmen. Now let me pass." They could see this fiery redhead meant business, so they moved their carriage. "Albert was a lucky man to have bedded that wild Irish beauty," one said to the other.

When Mary arrived home, she went to find Connor as she wanted to relax with him over a wine, as it had been a busy few days. The children were exhausted, Charles had found his legs so was walking everywhere and his siblings were his watchdogs. Mary enjoyed having the estate to themselves. She didn't like having servants, although Margaret would be here soon but she was family, so no gossip would be spread. As soon as Margaret was settled in, Mary and Connor would travel to Ireland and inspect some of the Rothchild farms. They had found maps in Albert's office of all the farms and where they were located. Once the children were fed, they played games with them until it was time for bed.

After settling the children down, they retired to the drawing room and sat together on the settee and had another wine. Tonight, Mary felt relaxed and happy, as she was able to share her wealth with her family, so poverty had gone from their lives forever. She hoped to be able to act fast on the farms as she wanted this all to happen before her father passed away. She wanted him to enjoy time back in his homeland, especially if it was on an Irish farm. As she thought of the happiness she had given her family, a warm feeling flowed through her body. For all this to have happened she had relied on Connor so much. His devotion to the children was amazing, but above all his patience waiting for her. Mary leaned over and put her arms around his waist and snuggled into him; she loved this young man to bits. When she got this close to him, a surge of emotions took over and she desperately wanted him to make love to her. Now was the time, she was ready for however much love he could give to her. Connor rose and took her hand and they ran to the bedroom together, pushed the door shut, raced to undress, with Connor being first as he had less clothes to remove. Mary grabbed him and pulled him close to her. She was still not fully undressed, but this didn't stop his manly parts from stirring and this sent tingling sensations through her body. She asked Connor to finish undressing her so she could caress him making him more excited. As Mary's body was revealed, Connor kissed her breasts while moving his hands smoothly down her body lingering on her womanly parts. Mary begged him to play with her as she lay on the bed enjoying the feelings that were surging through her body, arousing passion that she could no longer hold back. She reached out and pulled Connor on top of her, pleading with him to take her. They made passionate love among the bedclothes, stirring up a tangled mess, both letting out squeals of delight as their bodies became one. This was what love was all about, to make each other happy, to lay in each other's arms in silence, then drop off to sleep exhausted. This was the start of their life together. The past had been put behind Mary, she could now move on.

Margaret had arrived and was settled in, and it didn't take long for the children to bond with her. Tomorrow

Mary and Connor were leaving for Ireland. They were catching the train, then boarding the ferry to Queenstown, then travelling by train to Dunmanway in Cork. They had a map and all the property titles that they had been studying all night, also Albert's journal on the tenant farmers' names; these they were taking with them. Mary didn't know what to expect. She was only young when the family had left Ireland. She couldn't remember anything at all, so this was going to be a new experience.

As they arrived in Dunmanway, dusk was setting in so they booked into an inn for a night. This was the first time in Connor's life that he didn't have to worry about money so it was a new adventure for them both. They both fell into bed tired after a full day of travel. The next morning, they rose early and had breakfast, then hired a carriage for the day. They asked the driver to take them to the farms on the map that were marked. There were several near Dunmanway so they started with the nearest one. When they drove up to the first farm, Mary asked the driver to wait while she spoke to the tenant farmer. He was an Irish farmer and making a survivable living until recently when the land tariffs had been increased. "We know the price the landowners are getting for their wheat, it goes up all the time but all we get is an increase in land tariffs. We see none of the profits. They are getting richer while we are getting poorer. How are we meant to survive?" he asked Mary. She explained who she was and said she was going to take the increased taxes off her lands so they could have a better life. For this he was very grateful and thanked her. The next place they visited had an English farmer. He was somewhat different and didn't appreciate an Irish person enquiring about his farm. Mary took note of this; he would have to go. One of her brothers could go onto this farm.

The cottage was small but looked tidy. She marked this as farm number two. She gave the tenant one month to vacate the farm and he was not happy. He let her know he didn't like the Irish.

They stayed the night in the same inn and would move on tomorrow. The next morning they caught the train to Dublin then on to Dundalk, where they again hired a carriage. They asked the driver to take them to the farm they had marked on the map. He drove them there and pulled up at the gate. Mary went to the cottage and knocked on the door. A middle-aged man came to the door so Mary explained who she was. "Why have you increased our land tariffs? I have to walk off this farm. I have six mouths to feed, we can't survive so I'm leaving at the end of the month," and slammed the door in Mary's face. She knocked again to try to explain what she was going to do for her tenant farmers but he wouldn't open it. She was shocked to hear about these people's plight. Mary walked back to the carriage very despondent. She asked the carriage driver what the general feeling among the tenant farmers was. "The rents the landlords charge is excessively high, almost bordering on robbery. The poor farmers are under threat of permanent eviction without notice; even when they pay these extortionate rents, their futures are never secure, especially the Irish," he told them. Mary marked this as farm number three on the map; as it was becoming vacant, one of her brothers could farm this one. She had seen enough, she didn't want to see any more. It was time for action; she just wanted to get back to her estate and draw up new leases so her tenant farmers could survive. Now they understood a lot more about the plight of those farming the land. She realised that most of the tenant farmers were Irishmen, which the absentee owners could treat with contempt. They could screw them as they had nowhere else to go. A meagre living was better than starving. While Mary had been talking to the farmers, Connor was taking notes. He would come back with Mary's siblings and get them settled in.

Once back over the Irish Sea and now in Cornwall, they booked into an inn so they could talk to the family about the farms. The youngest son, Patrick, and his father would farm the Dunmanway farm and Daniel would farm at Dundalk, just past Dublin. This would be happening in a month's time so now they could notify their employer. Julia had arranged board so she could continue her education. Their father was happy to be leaving England; only one month to go and he would be back living in his homeland. He had waited many years for this to happen. He had never considered himself anything other than a true Irishman.

Mary and Connor were happy to be back on the estate with their children. Margaret was settling in and enjoying life as a land girl. She loved the outdoor work and between her and Mary, the estate gardens were looking picture perfect. They still used the conservatory to grow their plants from seeds, as there were plenty of damp days and this was the place to be in this cooler weather. Mary had lengthy talks with her solicitor about the tenant farmers' land tariffs. She wanted to know if the estate was making good profits before they increased the tariffs. He assured her they were, and Albert was against the raise but he had been outvoted. He wouldn't stand up against the gentry. He could have because he was the largest landowner, but that is what the gentry did, they stood united. "It was only when Albert met you, Mary, that he started to take notice how the Irish had suffered. The other gentry showed no mercy towards the Irish, they were there to make money for themselves so they could live a lavish lifestyle. They have probably never been to Ireland to see the suffering. Their Irish lands have been passed down through generations as inheritances, they will have no concept or really care about what is happening over the Irish Sea. I have been to Ireland, Mary, and seen it; it is sad. Absenteeism is a universal practice in Ireland and is detrimental to the country's progress." This made Mary unhappy to think the tariff increases were for greed. She told her solicitor that they had visited some of the farms and families were struggling since the increases. "I want to reduce the tariffs back to where they were, so families have a better chance of surviving." "You realise, Mary, this will bring about resentment from the gentry, but because you are the first Irish landowner to live among them, this could be the time to bring about change, you have nothing to lose. Albert would have liked to have done this, but he was of the older gentry," said the solicitor. They drew up new agreements with the tariffs reduced to their former amounts. This gave Mary some comfort knowing she was able to help her people stay on their farms.

As she was leaving the solicitor's office she was stopped by two of the gentry. "We believe you have been to Ireland," they said. "Yes, I have, and I was appalled by what I saw. I have just written new contracts to my tenant farmers and reduced their land tariffs." "You can't do that, Mary, we took a vote and the majority voted to raise the tariffs," they said. "But did you forget Alfred was against it?" "That was only because he was bedding you, Mary, he was blinded by love. You must be good in bed; show us how good you are?" With this Mary walked away; her dislike for the gentry was rising fast. She would not tell

Connor of this incident, she had not told him of the previous one. He would want revenge, he was Irish.

A couple of days later a carriage pulled up in front of their home. Connor attended to it as Mary was busy. Two men came to the door and asked for Mary. "She is busy at the moment. Can I help you?" he asked. "Why are you here?" they wanted to know. "I am a friend of Mary's. Can I give her a message?" They were both stuck for words, this they never expected. Was Mary bedding this man? He was another bloody Irishman. "Tell her we want to hold a board meeting here on Thursday." "Just a moment until I see if this is okay with her," and he walked away to check with Mary. She wouldn't come to the door, so Connor went back. "Yes, Mary said that would suit, come at two o'clock." With that they left without a thank you or a goodbye. As they walked away they noticed the grounds and gardens still looked beautiful. "This is a credit to Mary. Do you think that is her new bed-mate. Why would she choose a bloody Irishman when there are so many gentry willing to bed her?" they asked of each other.

Thursday had arrived and the carriages were pulling up at the front entrance. Mary and Margaret had been busy making hors d'oeuvre, as was always expected after a board meeting. Connor and Margaret would attend the gentry after the meeting in the drawing room. The chairperson welcomed everyone and said this was the first ever meeting of the gentry that had been attended by a lady. "We are here today to discuss the land tariffs of the tenant farmers. At our last meeting we took a vote and the majority here agreed to raise the tariffs. I have been informed that you, Mary, have gone against our ruling, is that right?" he asked. "Yes, that is right. I visited Ireland and our tenant farmers are struggling to survive. How can we justify putting up the tariffs when we don't increase their wheat payments? This is unfair," Mary replied. "But Mary, in business life isn't fair, you will have to learn this," was the reply. "I learnt the tariffs that us landlords charge are considered excessively high, in fact bordering on robbery. Did you know, landlords are thought of as non-productive parasites? This in itself is disgusting, I don't want to be known as a parasite, and that is why I have reduced my land tariffs to what they were before the raise. Ireland has been sacrificed to London but change is in the air. How many of you here have been to Ireland?" Only one hand was raised. "What was your opinion?" asked Mary. "I wouldn't go back," was all that was volunteered. The meeting went quiet, no-one was in a hurry to talk. "I'm sorry, gentlemen of the gentry, I am not going to be ruled by greedy men. I will make my own decisions and they will be in favour of the Irish tenant farmer. You can do what you like, as I will be doing." Again, the room went quiet. These men had never been spoken to by an outspoken woman before, let alone one of Irish stock. "Oh, one last thing before I leave this meeting: I would like to thank you for all your offers to bed me, but I am being bedded. I will take my leave. Drinks and hors d'oeuvre will be served in the drawing room," and Mary left. Silence reigned over the boardroom. What was then discussed behind closed doors after Mary left was not for her ears.

The gentry filed through to the drawing room, where Connor and Margaret were hosts. None of them had seen Margaret before but guessed she was Mary's sister, not as pretty but okay on the eye. Who was the man, was he the lucky one that was bedding Mary? Some brave gentry asked Connor what he did for a living. He thought for a moment. "I am Mary's minder." No more questions were asked. Suddenly a little toddler appeared among the gentry; Charles had made his way into the drawing room. "Well, if that isn't a young Albert," commented someone. They all turned to look at him. "Yes, that's a certainty," said another. With that Connor picked him up and took him away. He thought the English gentry were arrogant and was proud that Mary was standing her ground with them, not becoming part of their closed society.

As the gentry were leaving, they gathered at their carriages. There would have to be another meeting but they would tackle Mary from a different angle. She was crucial to their wheat exports as the freight charges that were imposed on goods imported into the United Kingdom were highly volatile, sometimes reaching three times the normal rate. United they had better bargaining power, therefore they could not afford to lose her.

A month had passed and Connor was on his way to help shift Mary's father and brothers back to Ireland. As they crossed the Irish Sea, Mary's father bid his final farewell to England. It was not his choice to come to England, he was forced to leave Ireland so he could feed his family, but now he was on his way home. The Dunmanway farm was the new home to Patrick and his father, as it was closer to his remaining siblings. The cottage was small but the two of them would be comfortable. The wheat crops were starting to shoot and there was enough land to grow potatoes. Each farmer liked to grow their staple diet — potatoes — to feed their families. Ireland had one of the highest average wheat yields in the world, due to its cool temperate climate and high annual rainfall. This is why the English held on to their inherited Irish lands, because they returned good incomes. Once Patrick was settled, Connor gave him money to buy a horse and cart and a little extra in case he needed to buy farm equipment. This was from Mary. The next day he and Daniel caught the train to Dundalk and then hired a carriage to take them to the farm. The cottage was left in a mess by the vacating tenant. It was a larger cottage but they had to spend the next day cleaning it. They worked hard to bring it up to an acceptable standard. The land was very fertile and the wheat was shooting. Connor gave Daniel money to buy a horse and cart so they did this and stocked up on food, then drove back out to the farm. Mary had given Connor this money to give her siblings to get them started. The siblings were grateful to be given a chance to be tenant farmers for such a fair landowner. It was up to them now! Connor stayed with Daniel for a week and he met his neighbours, who were only too willing to help guide him through the first season. They knew they were back in Ireland as people cared about each other, that's what the Irish were known for.

After leaving Daniel, Connor caught the train back to Dunmanway to see how Patrick and his father were settling in. Patrick came to the station to pick Connor up and when they reached the farm, there was Mary's father sitting outside in an old rocking chair. He was as happy as a little sandboy. His dream had been fulfilled, he could now die peacefully; he had come back to his homeland.

Mary was happy to have Connor home again, she missed not having his arms around her at nights. The children missed him too as they had no-one to help them spot the squirrels in the woods. He was able to tell Mary how her brothers were settling in and how grateful they were for this wonderful opportunity; to them it was freedom from a life in the mines. Her father, James, was at last living his dream, if only for a short time. She knew in her own heart it would not be for long, but his last wish was fulfilled. And sadly, that is what happened. A week later a carriage drove up the estate driveway and stopped at the front entrance. A policeman knocked at the door and when Margaret answered it she knew their father had passed away. She thanked him and went to find Mary to pass on the sad news. They cried in each other's arms, but the saving grace was that he had made it home. Mary and Margaret left the next morning to catch the train to Cornwall to pick up Julia and head across the Irish Sea. Connor stayed on at the estate to care for the children.

Patrick told the family what had happened. He came in from the paddocks one evening and his father was asleep in his rocking chair. He prepared tea and called him to come in, but there was no answer so he went out to wake him, but he had passed away. He fetched a blanket leaving him to complete his homecoming! Patrick had arranged with the local priest to hold a mass at the Catholic church in Dunmanway, so the three sisters stayed in the local inn. Daniel came down from Dundalk and stayed with Patrick. Three of James's siblings came to the mass to farewell their brother; they were all very elderly. The graveyard was adjacent to the church so when the mass finished the coffin was carried out of the church to where he was to be buried. They lay their mother's ashes with their father so they could be together again. It was common in Ireland to have graveyards in church grounds, and it was not unusual to see piles of stones instead of a headstone, as this was all the poor could afford, but they knew where their loved ones were buried. The family went back to the inn to celebrate their father's life and reflect how far they had all come, leaving behind their days of poverty and near starvation. There was a tinge of sadness as their sisters

Norah and Kate were not with them. No-one had heard from Kate, they didn't know anything of her life. Daniel was loving the farming life and had met a lovely Irish lass that he was serious about. All too soon they were saying their farewells to each other as they left for their respective homes.

7

Life on the Estate

Ten years had passed and Mary and Connor's family had grown. They now had twin boys whom they named after their fathers, Sean and James. Connor's surname was O'Leary. Rose was fourteen and was the spitting image of her mother. Joseph, now twelve, was definitely Connor's son as he had the trademark dimple, and Charles, he was the black sheep, Albert's black sheep, and was still the attention-seeking lad who thought life owed him. The twins were coming up seven, and easy to please. They just got on with life, although they were given a hard time by Charles who was forever teasing them about their red Irish hair. Of course, a lot of this came from school as their family were the only Irish family in the neighbourhood. All the other children were from English gentry families, so four redheads at the school bore the brunt of many

Irish jokes. Charles was ten years old when he learned at school that his father was Lord Albert Rothchild. It had never been talked about at home as a lord meant nothing to Mary or Connor. One day after Charles had been to one of the other estates for a friend's birthday, he came home and asked his mother, "Who is the lord in our family? My father was a lord and it has to pass on to one of his sons." Mary was taken back by this. She knew the title belonged in the family, but to whom? Yes, she knew it should go to Charles, as he was Albert's son, but legally on paper Joseph was the eldest son. Neither Connor nor Mary wanted Joseph to have the title as he was Irish, not English, so this subject was never talked about. But now it had surfaced and wouldn't go away. "You know, Charles, that the title goes to the first-born son, who is Joseph," Mary told him. "But I am named Charles after my grandfather. He was a lord so it should come to me. The other kids are Irish, look at their red hair. I am the one who is English," he pointed out to his mother. "Your sister and your brothers inherited their genes from my Irish family, it doesn't mean they are not English," said Mary. "But the kids at school said I should be the lord," he said adamantly. Mary told him it would not be discussed again, he was too young to be worrying about a title. Charles was livid, why should the title go to Joseph? He didn't even look English. It was him, Charles, that looked like his father and grandfather. Mary could see a battle looming in the future over this lord business, not from anyone other than Charles. From this day forth he distanced himself from his brother, and this upset Connor and Mary as they had given the same love to each of their children.

They faced a dilemma. The only way the title could go to Charles by law was if Joseph was an illegitimate son of

Albert's, this indeed being true but it would cause such a scandal, and how the gentry loved a scandal. Because Mary had stuck to her guns with the Irish land tariffs there was still tension with the gentry towards her, and that she had chosen an Irishman to bed her added salt to the wound. Why didn't she choose one of them, when they were all eager to bed her? They were the English gentry, to them there really was no other choice! She was known among them as the hot Irish beauty and was still the most talked about subject, with hope that she would still be available one day ... but for whom?

Charles excelled at school. He was a brilliant scholar and was popular among his peers; he was certainly his father's child. His siblings were average at school, they had no standout qualities, they were just ordinary kids who loved life. At times, Joseph felt hurt the way his brother treated him — although he was the eldest, he was not the smartest. All the children loved going into the woods to look for squirrels and sometimes they would see the sly old fox. Connor had bought some chickens for Rose, and had built her a henhouse as she wanted to look after the hens and collect their eggs. One morning she found a half-eaten chicken outside the henhouse; it had been eaten by a fox. She came into the home crying so Connor went to the tool-shed and got his gun and went on a fox hunt but to no avail. He put the gun back out of the reach of the children. A couple of days later Charles went into the tool-shed and climbed up and lifted the gun down. He had watched Connor put the bullet in so decided to have a go. He knew it was wrong for him to touch the gun but this was Charles, rules weren't made for him. At the same time, Joseph walked into the tool-shed to get something and there was a loud bang. He fell to the ground. Charles ran to the home calling for help as there had been an accident. Mary came running to the shed only to see Joseph lying in a pool of blood. She yelled for Connor to get the carriage and when he saw his son he ran to him and picked him up. Someone came with a blanket and they wrapped it around him, then they put him in the carriage to take him to the hospital.

It was a waiting game as they sat huddled together until the doctor came to them with the news that Joseph was very badly injured. They sat with their arms around each other both in tears, willing Joseph to stay with them. It suddenly dawned on Connor what had happened — he had been shot, but how? The gun was out of the children's reach. Joseph would not have touched the gun, was it Charles who had the gun? Connor felt responsible, but he had told the children they were never to touch the gun without him being there. Joseph was the child that was conceived out of unfinished love by Mary and Connor, he was who had reunited them. They were asked to come into a room where the doctor was and were given the news they never wanted to hear: Joseph had passed away. The bullet had pierced his heart. They tried to comfort each other but this was devastating. Their eldest son, born from absolute love, had only been lent to them for a short time, twelve years. He had been given all the love needed in that time by his family.

They drove home in silence, neither knowing what to say, there wasn't really anything to say, the pain was too great. What would they tell the other children? What had happened in the shed? Who had the gun? They would have to ask Charles; would he be forthcoming with the truth? As they pulled up at the entrance, Margaret came out with Rose and the twins, and she knew that something terrible had happened by the pain displayed on Mary and Connor's faces. They went inside to the drawing room, but where was Charles? Connor went to his room and he was sitting on his bed reading. He asked him to come to the drawing room. Mary told them that Joseph would not be coming home as he had passed away. Everyone burst into tears and hugged each other, all except Charles. He just sat with a blank look on his face. "Tell us what happened, Charles, who had the gun?" asked Connor. "Joseph got it down and put the bullet in it, I went to take it off him and the gun went off." "But you both knew you were not allowed to touch the gun, that is why it was put out of your reach," said Connor. With this Charles got up and left the room. No-one had seen what happened. Was this the truth?

It as a sad household. The children and especially Rose were badly affected by the sudden loss of their brother, but the one suffering most was Connor. He loved his eldest son and refused to think he would have touched the gun when he knew he was told not to, this was not in Joseph's makeup. Charles had told him otherwise, but a suspicion in the back of Connor's mind lingered ... who really had the gun? Because both Mary and Connor were not ready to bury any of their children, it had never been discussed. As they both called Ireland home they had to seriously think where they were going to settle when they grew older, as they couldn't bear the thought of Joseph in England if they settled in Ireland. Connor was an Irishman through and through and Mary knew it would call him home one day. They decided to take Joseph home to Ireland and bury him next to his grandfather James, in Dunmanway. England had been good to Mary but she knew one day she would have to leave the estate. If she didn't live here, then she would go back to her Irish roots.

Margaret helped Mary and Connor take the children to Ireland. She hadn't left the estate yet to find another position as she was happy working on her sister's estate. This was the children's first visit to the homeland, and they were excited as well as sad. Patrick had arranged for the funeral to be held in the little church in Dunmanway. The coffin had gone on before them so it was waiting there at the funeral parlour. Mary's brothers and their families came to the church for the service and they all celebrated Joseph's life, then he was buried by his grandfather. He would never be alone or forgotten. Charles complained all the time wanting to go back to the estate; he hated Ireland. No-one could understand why he didn't shed a tear for Joseph; it seemed as if he hadn't lost his brother. Mary and Connor had decided that after the family went back to England they would get a headstone made with 'Joseph O'Leary', not 'Rothchild', on it, as that was his rightful name. Explanations would have to come later when the sadness had gone. One day when the time was right they would explain to Rose about her rightful name and she could make a choice, although when she married, her name would change, so it really wasn't so important for her. Now, of course, the way was clear for Charles to become Lord Charles Rothchild, as he was the eldest living son.

8

The Way Forward

It took a long time for Connor and Mary to get over losing Joseph. There was still an air of doubt surrounding his death, as Connor could not bring himself to believe it was Joseph who had fired the gun. The police had interviewed Charles, who told the same story, that he tried to take the gun off Joseph, then it went off. Charles was distancing himself from the family but Mary thought it was because he had witnessed Joseph's death. Connor felt estranged from him, but because he was Mary's son he had to treat him as if he was his own, otherwise they might have fallen apart as a family. Deep down he couldn't shake off the resentment he held for him, but he couldn't tell Mary as she was suffering enough.

Rose was having her fifteenth birthday party at the estate. She had asked five of her friends home for tea. This was the first celebration in the family since losing Joseph, so Mary and Connor knew they had to put their sadness behind them and celebrate with Rose. She was a beautiful girl with her mother's red hair, and her ambition was to be a schoolteacher. Although she wasn't brainy, she would persevere with her schoolwork because she had a goal to achieve, she had her mother's fight. Margaret had put in an all-out effort to make the food special for this day. Rose's friends were all daughters of the gentry, as they lived in this area and attended the school she went to. It wasn't by choice that Mary chose this school for the children but it was the one that served their area. She and Connor were not of gentry standing, they weren't part of that scene, but in spite of this, the neighbours were cordial to them. Board meetings by the gentry were still held occasionally but only when they needed Mary's agreement on some matter. They knew she wouldn't enter into any tariff increases; they were off limits to the gentry. If decisions had to be made on the exporting of wheat, then they needed her, being the largest producer, but Mary's mind was made up on this subject and she would not budge ... her countrymen came first.

Rose asked Connor if he would take her and the girls into the woods later looking for squirrels, as she loved doing this. She still didn't know he was her birth father, this secret had not been revealed ... but any day now! Mary and Connor would tell her but they didn't want Charles to know for fear of him telling everyone; this would be devastating for Rose, especially among the gentry. The twins, of course, were known to belong to Connor because they were born after Albert died, so this was acceptable. But Rose's secret, if it got out, would take away her share of the estate, Mary thought, thus leaving Charles and Mary as joint owners, but with his title of Lord it gave him advantages. Rose's share was vital to Mary. She could see once Charles became Lord Charles Rothchild, it would go to his head and he would side with the gentry, as that is what he fancied himself as. He would not be sympathetic to the plight of the Irish, therefore Mary's good work would be undone.

Carriages rolled up with the girls for Rose's party. They were all of the gentry. Rose took them for a walk around the gardens and they thought they were beautiful so she told them her mother grew all the plants and showed them the conservatory where they were propagated. Then she called to Connor and asked him to please take them into the woods for a squirrel hunt. They had never done anything like this before and squealed with delight when they found one. Rose chased it, as she loved watching it scamper up the bark of the tree and nestle in the branches, then it would sit there watching them. Its long bushy tail hung down like a fluffy feather duster. In all they found six squirrels so each girl had a chance to chase one. Their fathers never did spend any recreational time with them, being daughters of the gentry, so this was an adventure for them. Mary called for them to come and eat. There was plenty of food on the table for the girls to choose from. Sean and James lined up but Charles was nowhere to be seen. Mary went to his room, as she wanted him to join in Rose's birthday celebrations, but he was not there. They would just have to start without him. When most of the food was gone, Margaret brought out the cake for Rose to blow out her candles, all fifteen of them, then make a wish. "I want to share my wish with everyone here today," said Rose as she closed her eyes. "Joseph, wherever you are I miss you, especially today, but I think of you every day. We all miss you, God bless." Then she blew out the candles. They all sang and wished her a happy birthday. Mary and Connor could not believe what Rose had just done, shared her birthday wish with all her friends. Connor was so proud of her, he wanted to tell her right there and then he was her birth father as it broke his heart that she didn't know, but one day she would. When they had finished eating the girls all filed into Rose's room and did what teenage girls did. Later on, Connor and Rose delivered the girls home in their carriage and they all thanked him for taking them squirrel hunting. As they were driving home, Rose leaned over and kissed Connor on the cheek. "The girls think I am lucky to have such a kind stepfather. They loved my party, so thank you, father." Connor put his arms around her and told her he loved her dearly, more than she would ever know!

When the leftover party food was being gathered up, Charles turned up to start feasting. Mary was so angry with him. "Why weren't you here to celebrate with your family, especially for Rose? She is your sister, this was her fifteenth birthday." "I didn't want to be around silly giggly girls so I went for a walk," was his answer. "Well, you can walk straight to your room right now without any food," replied an angry Mary. "I hate this family!" he yelled. Connor followed him and grabbed him. "Don't ever talk like that again, young man." "I'm glad I look English like my father, one day I will be an English lord," he told them. With this Connor slapped his face as images of his beloved Joseph flashed before his eyes. All Connor could see was Charles getting his own way, taking over the estate now that Joseph was gone, the way was clear for him. Connor was so angry he went to their room and lay on the bed and let his tears flow. This was where Mary found him and she lay with him and they cried together.

After this episode Charles demanded to go to boarding school. He didn't want to live with his family any more, he wanted a proper English education. Mary tried to talk him into staying with them but he was adamant he was going to boarding school, his mind was made up. She wondered where it all went wrong with Charles but reflecting back on his upbringing, it all started with Albert telling Mary to pick him up every time he cried. She remembered telling Albert he would become the spoilt child always demanding attention, and this is what had happened. Connor didn't try to persuade him otherwise as he thought a bit of strict discipline would straighten him out. Hopefully boarding school would teach him some manners!

9

Six Years Later

Charles was now sixteen and was coming home from boarding school for the school holidays. He had excelled at school and was now a head student at the college. Everyone was on edge as their happy family life was going to be turned upside down, as always happened when he came home. He bossed the twins around and teased them about their red hair. They were now thirteen. Rose was twenty-one and after the school holidays she was starting a teaching position at the local school. She had worked hard and passed all her exams and was now joining the workforce. Her parents were so proud of her. One of the gentry sons was taking her out. She was very popular with the boys, egged on by their fathers, as Rose Rothchild would be a good catch as her family were very wealthy.

Mary had taken the carriage to the train station to pick up Charles. He put his bags inside the carriage and Mary asked him to ride up front with her so she could talk to him while driving home. He refused, saying he would sit in the carriage; he didn't want to be seen being driven home by his mother, that was beneath him. This hurt Mary as she wanted to discuss things with him. She could see things hadn't changed, he was still the pompous child that he always was. She wondered what Albert would have thought of him. Would he have been as disappointed as she felt?

When they arrived home, Mary alighted from the carriage and walked around to give him a cuddle, but he just walked away. "Charles, come back here and give me a cuddle," she asked. "I don't need cuddles, I'm grown up now, I'm an adult." Connor was watching and saw the hurt in Mary's eyes. "It doesn't matter how old you are, Charles, have the decency to at least give your mother a cuddle, she has missed you," he said. He fired Connor the most distasteful look, then gave his mother a hug and walked off with his bag. The twins came running up to him to ask him about boarding school. "Get out of my way, gingernuts," he told them. This was too much for Connor. He grabbed Charles from the back and turned him around. "Come here, boys," he told the twins. "Now what do you want to ask your brother?" They said they just wanted to know if it was hard learning at boarding school. "Right, Charles, answer your brothers." "It's not hard for me because I am smart," he said. With this Connor let him go. He could feel no love for this child. He wondered why Joseph was taken and not Charles!

That night at supper Charles sat next to Rose and Sean. "Guess what, Charles? I start my teaching at the beginning of next term, I'm so excited," she said. "Why would anyone be excited about just being a teacher?" he asked. "Your mother and I are proud of you, Rose," said Connor.

Rose felt deflated with Charles's answer. "What are you going to be?" she asked Charles. "Oh, I'm going to be an estate lawyer, I've already started my degree. I'm learning all about estates and titles, which reminds me, I am applying for father's title of Lord, as I am the eldest son. That will give me more power at college and I can attend the gentry gentlemen's club when I'm twenty-one." Connor looked at Mary in disbelief and left the table. "Look what you have done, Charles, your father has left the table because of your insensitive talk. Do you not remember you had a brother who was taken from us? He was the eldest child and all you can think of is the bloody title," said a tearful Mary. "Mother, that happened six years ago, life moves forward, get over it," he answered. "Leave this table now, Charles!" she yelled. He wasn't even home one day and he had caused an upset. The next day no-one saw him and he was left to his own devices, so began a peaceful day. Connor was teaching the twins how to handle the horses and drive the cart and carriage. He wanted them to have their independence. They were keen to learn, they were hands-on boys and loved being with their father, and in turn he loved being with them. There was no self-righteousness with them, they were down-to-earth lads. Rose could handle the horse and carriage and often went to town on her own. She spent a lot of time in the conservatory with her mother learning how to grow plants, as so many people commented on their beautiful gardens. Charles never appeared all day, and no-one bothered him.

That night as Mary and Connor lay in bed, they wondered when the right time would be to tell Rose the truth as to who her father was. Also, there was the matter of the estate. On reaching twenty-one years of age, the children would get a share of Albert's estate, and now Rose was of age. She and Charles shared half of the estate and Mary had the other half. Thank goodness Albert had named the children to whom the estate went to. If it ever got out that Rose was not Albert's child, as long as she was named nothing could happen. Mary had found out from the solicitor about this and he confirmed as long as she was named then nothing could change. He also told Mary there was a substantial amount of money sitting in the estate, and was there anything she wanted to buy? She discussed it with Connor and they both agreed that it be put in a separate bank account, as they could foresee problems arising in the future once Charles had the title of Lord. They wanted to protect their future and not let their Irish tenant farmers down, but would Charles give a damn? Hardly! As long as Rose retained a share, she and Mary had the controlling interest, so they could outvote Charles. Mary and Connor lay in each other's arms wondering what to do next. Mary snuggled up to him and felt that familiar feeling welling up in her heart. She pulled him tight into her body and caressed his back and buttocks. It wasn't long before she knew he was eager to take her. She loved Connor to bits and his response told her he felt the same for her. Their love had never waned, the excitement and passion was as strong now as it was back in that bathroom in the London lodgings all those years ago. Rose was a pleasant reminder, and what a beautiful souvenir they were gifted.

10

Secrets Unveiled

Mary, Connor and Rose were on their way to Ireland. The other children were at home on the estate with Margaret. This was a special treat for Rose for her twenty-first birthday and for qualifying for her teaching position. That night they arrived in Dunmanway and were booked in at the inn. Rose was going to be told a lot of truths on this holiday, truths that would change her life forever! They settled in for the night as they were tired. Tomorrow they would feel fresh and the first place they were taking Rose was to Joseph's grave. After breakfast they decided to walk to the church as it was a nice day. They talked about Joseph and the happy memories he had left them with, it was as if he had never left. When they arrived at the churchyard Mary asked Rose to find Joseph's grave and read the headstone. They both stood back and watched what happened. Rose walked to where she remembered where he was buried. There before her stood a beautiful headstone, but why did it have 'Joseph O'Leary'? He was Joseph Rothchild. She stood still, then she felt arms surrounding her. Beside her stood Mary and Connor, both with tears streaming down their cheeks. "Mother, why is 'Joseph O'Leary' on the headstone?" she asked. "Because, my darling, he was Connor's child, not Albert's, but no-one knew this except the two of us. Come and sit down, we have something we want to tell you." They walked over to a seat and Rose sat between them. "I don't know where to start but perhaps if I go to the beginning," said Mary. She sat and held her hand as she told Rose the whole story of her and Connor, then meeting Albert. When Mary finished, Rose was sobbing. "What a beautiful story," and she turned to Connor and hugged him. "I always wanted you to be my father. So my name is O'Leary, not Rothchild?" "Well, Rose, you are a Rothchild on all the records, but in your heart, we know you are an O'Leary," Mary told her. "Does that mean Charles is not my real brother?" she asked. "Yes, he is your half-brother, but the twins are your true brothers as was Joseph." "Oh mother, I'm glad Charles is not my true brother, he is so mean to all of us about our Irish traits," she said. "Rose, we want this to be kept between ourselves. In Albert's will you were named along with Joseph and Charles as beneficiaries, so you and I can outvote Charles. I can see problems arising when he becomes a lord — he will have more power than any of us. But together we are in control as he will side with the gentry, then all I have worked for to protect our Irish tenant farmers will be lost. Our people suffered, Rose, my own mother died of starvation to feed her family. I made a promise to myself that I would protect our people, this I will do until my dying day," Mary said passionately. "I know how passionate you and father are about the Irish, it has come through in my veins, and now I know why. I am totally Irish, no English blood at all, that is such a surprise!" "Are you sad with what you have learnt today, Rose?" asked Connor. "No, father, I am happy to find out that I am Irish and that the twins are my blood brothers. I am proud of my mother for all she has done to make a better life for her people as well as her family. I will do the same as they are my people now, and most of all to find out you are my true father, how good is that?" sobbed Rose. "Thank you, my darling Rose," said Mary.

Next visit was to see Patrick and his family. He now had an Irish wife and three children and they loved living on the farm. None of Mary's siblings had forgotten their Irish roots or the opportunity Mary had given them. She was their saviour! Mary was the brave one of the family, she wanted a better life and went searching for it. No-one had heard from Kate since she left for New Zealand. She had now become a distant memory but was never forgotten. Her family hoped she had found a new life and a new beginning in a distant land. One small grace was that she didn't go on her own; her uncle Jeremiah Foley who was thirty-five also wanted to leave Ireland to find work. Immigration to New Zealand was being offered to family members so they pretended they were brother and sister, travelling on the ship *Waikato* under the name of Jeramiah and Mary Foley.

While spending four days in Dunmanway, Rose could not get over the poverty she saw. She loved the people and the vast countryside; it was not manicured like the English countryside, it was untamed. She felt a warmth tinged with sadness, but a feeling that would one day she would be drawn back. She shared her parents' love for the Irish, they were a humble race and very protective. Even among the poverty they could still manage a smile and a greeting, this Rose loved most about them. One night they went to a little pub for supper. Music from the Irish flute and violin floated through to where they were dining. It was beautiful, so when they finished they were drawn to where it was coming from. They found a crowded bar where people were singing and playing instruments; some were dancing and others were sitting enjoying their pints. It was a great atmosphere. One would never find this in England unless it was in an Irish bar. Comradeship was deep-rooted within the Irish culture, it was a sense of belonging. It wasn't long before Rose was approached by a young Irishman asking her to dance. She went with him and they found a space, then he took her in his arms and twirled her around and around until they burst into laughter. She couldn't believe the warmth she felt from this young man; this had never happened before, although she was going with the son of a gentry. He held her close to him; this was the hot Irish blood, the feeling of not holding back, but expressing what one felt at that moment. Mary and Connor watched as Rose danced with this young man. She reached across for Connor's hand, this was her life all over, that first moment she met him and how she dreamt of him for months, even years, that memory never leaving her. When Rose and the young man finished dancing they came back to their table and he asked if he could buy them drinks. They sat together talking and he told them a little about his family and his life. He was the only son of a tenant farmer. Their landlord was an absentee English gentry, but a good one as their land tariffs had been raised but were now reduced so they were able to make a living again. His father was not well so he had taken over the farm and he was grateful for this opportunity. Mary asked, "Do you know who your landlord is?" "Yes, it is a Lord Rothchild, but I think he died and it is taken over by his family," he answered. Mary looked at Rose with a smile but nothing more was said. "Can you make enough off the land to live a moderate life?" asked Connor. "Yes, we can, but our neighbours struggle as they have greedy landlords. They can't complain because they would be evicted with nowhere to go. We are blessed," he said. This left Mary and Connor feeling they were doing something to make life a little easier for the Irish; greed had not taken over. They thanked the young man for sharing his time with them. "Will you be here tomorrow night?" he asked Rose. "Yes, we are here for another night." "Can I see you again?" he asked. Rose agreed as she was intrigued. "Goodbye, my English rose," he yelled as they left. This brought tears to Mary's eyes; she was Albert's Irish rose and her daughter was the English rose. "What a nice young man," said Connor. "Tonight gave me a sense of belonging. One day I will come back, these are my people," said Rose. "Yes, my darling, when the time comes it will call us back home," agreed Mary.

Rose had learnt so much from tonight. She felt feelings stir in her body, nothing to do with the young man, she told herself, it was to do with the Irish and Ireland in general. There didn't seem to be any such thing as competition, just to be alive was enough to bring joy to these people. But then she did enjoy the company of the young man, he was so warm, in fact she was looking forward to tomorrow night. It was only then she realised she didn't know his name. They spent the next day sightseeing and everywhere they went they were greeted by strangers, thus making them feel welcome. Their last place to call today was the churchyard. Mary wanted to say a prayer for her father, then of course they as a family would grieve for Joseph. They stopped at a little stall and bought flowers to put by the headstones. It was especially sad for Connor as he missed his son. He still had bad feelings about who had the gun, and how the accident happened. Because Joseph stood in the way of Charles becoming Lord, was this the way to take him out? This thought wouldn't leave him. He would never have let Joseph have the lordship because he wasn't English, but of course Charles didn't know this. But, unfortunately, it ended there on that fateful day.

Tonight, they went back to the little pub. There waiting for Rose was her dancing partner, he had a table reserved for them. They greeted each other and Connor bought drinks for them. The music was in full swing, the party had begun, this was just a typical night in an Irish pub, he told them. He introduced himself as Brendon Carey. "How did you know my name?" Rose asked him. "I'm sorry but I don't know your name," he answered. "But you said goodbye, my English rose, last night. My name is Rose." With this they all laughed. "Come, Rose, time for us to dance?" Away they went together, and this time he was content to dance with her in his arms, holding her close. He had dreamt of her all last night. She looked Irish and so did her parents, but they said they were from England, they even spoke like the English. He had to ask her: "Are you not Irish?" "My parents were originally from Ireland but my mother's family left when she was young as there was no work for them in Ireland. My brother Joseph is buried here in the churchyard alongside my grandfather."

"What happened to him?" asked Brendon. "He and my stepbrother were playing with a gun and it went off and Joseph died. It devastated our family." "But why bury him here and not where you live?" he asked. "My family will come back and settle in Ireland, this is where their roots are, they couldn't leave him in England. My uncle is a tenant farmer here, he visits Joseph and his father, my grandfather." "Who is your uncle?" Brendon wanted to know. Rose told him it was Patrick Nyhan. That was enough questions, he thought, but then he had just one more: "What do you do, Rose?" She told him she had just qualified as a schoolteacher and that was why her parents had brought her here as a treat. Why couldn't she be staying longer? Brendon thought to himself, as he was really taken with her. They shared stories and had lots of laughs. Mary and Connor decided to call it a night so said their farewells to Brendon before walking back to the inn. He promised to see Rose back safely.

Rose and Brendon sat and shared stories over a couple more drinks, between singing along with the crowd. Rose had never had such fun; this was so different to the stuffy English pubs. She never told Brendon it was her family that owned his farm for fear of his walking away. He was such fun, full of joy and contentment for his life, one that he was grateful for, even though he farmed as a tenant farmer. They walked back to the inn hand in hand. When Rose was about to go inside he took her in his arms and kissed her passionately on the lips, pulling her close to him. She could feel a chemistry between them and put her arms around his neck. They kissed each other with their bodies touching and he could feel the closeness of her breasts. Then Rose remembered her mother's story so suddenly broke away. "I'm sorry if I upset you, Rose, I shouldn't have been so forward," he said, as he was angry with himself. "It's a long story, Brendon, but I really enjoyed tonight, you are the nicest guy I have ever met. One day we may meet again," she said as she opened the door and went inside. He just stood there not believing what he had just done. Never before had he gone so far with someone on their first date, but she seemed to want it to happen as much as he did. Just as well Rose broke away when she did or the consequences might have been a lot different.

The next day they caught the train to Dundalk to visit Daniel and his family. They, like Patrick, were grateful to Mary for rescuing them from a life of misery and struggle. The farm had been kind to them and afforded them a good life. Patrick had married the young lass he had met when they came over for their father's burial. They now had three children. It was bonding time for them and Rose read to the children and they loved her in return. They spent three days having a look around the area; it didn't seem to have suffered as much as Cork in the potato famine.

The next day they were on their way home. Rose was a little quiet today. Mary wondered if she was missing Brendon and hoped she hadn't make the same mistake as she had, but Rose had a career in front of her; all Mary had was the thought of starvation and poverty and how to escape it. They had all enjoyed their visit to Ireland and were sad it had come to an end.

What lay in front of them on their return to the estate? The twins would be happy to have their parents and Rose home. Charles had stirred up trouble most days as he was bored on the estate. He wasn't interested in the horses or the gardens. The twins loved hitching the carriage or the cart up to the horses and driving around the estate. One day they had gone into the tool-shed to get something and they found Charles with the gun in his hands. He pointed it at them and went 'bang'. They were frightened and ran and told Margaret what had happened. Margaret came out straight away only to find the gun was up on the rack. When she tackled Charles about it he denied what the boys had said, but she knew who to believe ... it wasn't Charles. She found him to be arrogant and he would have nothing to do with the twins other than to tease them. Margaret would be glad when he went back to boarding school, but she would certainly be telling Connor about the gun incident when they arrived home.

The twins' first assignment with the carriage was to drive it to the station to pick up their parents and Rose. They felt proud. They were all happy to see each other so there were hugs all round. Rose hugged the boys with special thoughts in her mind now that she knew they were her blood brothers; the three of them were Connor's children, they were special! Charles was another matter, he was all for himself, a stuck-up kid thinking he was someone special; the sad reality, he would be one day. Connor let the boys drive them home so he could see how they handled everything; they did just fine. Now he knew he could let them go into town together. As they pulled up at the front entrance Margaret was there to welcome them home. Charles was nowhere to be seen. Mary called to him but to no avail. While they unpacked Mary heard Rose telling Margaret about the lovely Irish lad she had meet and his name was Brendon. She had such fun in Ireland, she loved the Irish people. "I'm going back perhaps to teach one day," she said. Mary listened in and was surprised; had Rose left something behind in Dunmanway ... perhaps her heart!

Life was settling back to normal on the estate. Tomorrow Charles was leaving for boarding school so Margaret elected to tell Connor and Mary about the gun episode. They were horrified, fancy frightening the younger boys by pointing the gun at them. Connor was furious; he left the room to find Charles. He knocked on his bedroom door and walked in without being asked to come in. "Margaret just told me about you pointing the gun at the twins, what the hell have I told you about touching the gun?" Charles stood up with his hands on his hip. "It is their word against mine." Connor went up to him and kicked his backside. "I'm not going to say what I am thinking, but your smart tongue will land you in trouble one day, my lad," said an angry Connor. With this Charles told him to leave his room. Connor could not get out quick enough otherwise he might have had a murder on his hands. Suddenly old wounds surfaced as he thought about Joseph. What really did happen?

The next morning Charles was catching the train back to boarding school. No-one wanted to go to the station with him so Mary took him by herself. She wasn't upset, as she didn't blame the twins for not wanting to come. She asked Charles why he frightened the boys with the gun and he said it was just a joke. "That was a stupid joke, especially with the boys losing their brother." "He was only their half-brother," came back his answer. Tears welled up in Mary's eyes; if only he knew the truth, she thought. At the station they said their goodbyes. He walked off without giving his mother a hug, and this hurt her. Mary decided seeing she was in town she would go and see her solicitor and see that the land tariffs were all being paid. He told her he had transferred a large amount of money into her and Connor's bank account. "By the way, Mary, I had a visit from Charles. He asked me to proceed with the title of Lord as he would like it while at boarding school as it would give him more power. He would like to think he was someone, that lad. He also wanted to have a look at the financials on the estate, which he had no rights to until he was twenty-one. I told him so and that you owned half the estate and the other half was divided between him and Rose, now that Joseph was gone. He wanted to know what rights he had to the estate when he became Lord Charles Rothchild." "What did you tell him?" asked Mary. "The only privilege it gave him was to attend the gentry board meetings which allowed him a vote." "Will I still be able to vote?" Mary asked. "I'm not sure on that, Mary, perhaps it is only one vote from each estate but I will check up on this," said the solicitor. "By the way, now that Rose is a shareholder being twenty-one, money should be put into a separate account for her for the next few years until Charles comes of age. He is going to want his pound of flesh." "Yes, please arrange for that to happen, Rose deserves what is rightfully hers," said Mary with a divided heart on this matter. She could see a battle arising in the future and things would get nasty. Charles had certainly turned into one of the blue-blooded greedy English gentry. What would his father have thought of him? But deep in her heart she knew he would never have put his son before her, as he dearly loved his beautiful Irish rose.

But would she have remained with Albert, or would her love for Connor have taken her? That would never be known! Mary often thought about her situation if Albert had not got sick and passed away. Could she have walked out on him knowing it would have broken his heart? Either way, someone was going to be deeply hurt. As Mary drove home she was furious that Charles had gone behind her back; fancy trying to look into the estate finances, it was as if he didn't trust his own mother. This made her all the more determined to take out of the estate every cent that was hers until he was of age. She didn't know whether to tell Connor, as his feelings for Charles were nearly zilch; perhaps at a later date.

Today Rose began her teaching position at the local school. The twins were able to drive her each day as they were at the same school. She was excited. Her parents were proud of her even if Charles wasn't, but his opinion didn't matter any more, now she knew the truth. She had broken off with her gentry boyfriend since coming back from holiday and he was bitterly disappointed. His parents, especially his father, was keen for this romance to blossom, as he had seen the happiness her mother had brought Lord Albert; to have such a beauty in the family would be most welcome. They hounded the poor lad to make amends with Rose but it was not going to happen. She couldn't rid the happy memories of her time with Brendon and the warmth she felt, while in his arms. She was definitely her mother's daughter; the Irish were warm, beautiful people and so passionate. Rose saw it at home every day with her mother and father; she knew when they went to their room sometimes during the day, that they lay in each other's arms.

Margaret had applied for a position as a land-girl on a farm in the remote Scottish Highlands. The farm was a tenanted farm as were most of the farms and these people were known as 'crofters'. All she knew was that it was at 'Kyle of Lochalsh' on the Lochalsh peninsula on the northwest coast of Scotland, one hundred miles from Inverness. Because the Highlands were so isolated and the crofters were politically powerless, they turned to religion for comfort. Roman Catholicism was strong in remote locations as the Franciscan missionaries made the effort to cross the sea from Ireland to celebrate mass. The Irish potato fungus had reached the Scottish Highlands in 1846 and caused great distress.

This was going to be a challenge for Margaret but it was time for her to leave the Rothchild estate. She detested the way Charles treated his family. Ever since she reported him to Connor over the gun incident with the twins, it was as if she didn't exist. She had never seen this spoilt behaviour before and really felt for Mary and Connor, as he was treated no different to the other children. She had never met Lord Albert so didn't know if this was a family trait, but she could see trouble brewing. She was excited about the prospect of a new life in a remote area; it would be a challenge. She thought back to Mary when she left the family and went to London to seek a better life and look where it had taken her!

When the letter arrived telling Margaret she had the position and could start at the beginning of the next month, she was nervous but happy. Mary would miss her but this was Margaret's decision. They only had two weeks together before she left and everyone was going to miss her, that was, all except one person ... Charles!

11

Brendon

What of Brendon? He had tried to let go of his feelings for Rose, but she lingered in his heart. He had dated other girls but to no avail, they weren't right for him, there was nothing there. Then one day he met someone he quite liked and they went together for a year but he could not bring himself to bed her. She was ready but he was not. He didn't want the consequences in case she became with child and he found he didn't love her. He remembered Rose's uncle's name, Patrick Nyhan, so went to the titles office to find out where he lived, then drove his cart to his farm. He saw someone out in the wheat paddock so walked over and approached him. "Excuse me, Mr Nyhan, I am seeking some information. I met a young lady called Rose about two years ago who I belief to be your niece. Could you please give me her address as I want to write to her?" he asked. Patrick was surprised that this young man still remembered her after two years. "How long ago did you say since you met her?" Patrick asked. "I met her with her parents at the pub when they were visiting about two years ago. She has never left my mind. I would like to make contact with her," said Brendon. With this Patrick gave the young lad Rose's address; he must be keen! Then he asked him what he did for a living. He told Patrick he was a tenant farmer for the English gentry, and they were very fair landlords. "Who are your landlords?" asked Patrick. "I think it is the family of the late Lord Rothchild, they have kept the tariffs down so we can at least make a living from the land." "Did you know Lord Rothchild married an Irish lass and when he died she became the landlord? It is her who is looking after us Irish, she is my landlord too," said Patrick. "Well, well fancy that, aren't we lucky?" replied Brendon. Obviously, he did not know who Rose and her family were, they mustn't have told him. "Nice to have met you, young man, good luck in reaching your Rose," he said as he shook Brendon's hand. "Keep in touch and let me know how it all goes?" "I will, thank you, mister," and he drove off. Patrick could hardly hide his laughter; what a shock he was in for, if this friendship progressed. That night Brendon sat down and wrote Rose a letter. Goodness, he thought, her surname is Rothchild, it must be a common name in London. Then there was the address of an estate. Perhaps she boards there, that was the only answer he could think of.

When Rose arrived home from school one afternoon there was a letter waiting for her. She could see it had come from Ireland, but other than her uncles, who would be writing to her? She sat down and opened it and read the first line, then she knew. It began: 'My dear English rose. I have tried to forget you many times but you will not take leave from my heart ....' Rose could read no further;

she clutched the letter to her breast. She knew this very feeling. She ran to her room and sprawled out on her bed still clutching the letter. She was so excited she just had to read on. Then the tears started, it was such a beautiful letter. Brendon had remembered her. Rose hadn't bothered dating any of the young gentry, much to the annoyance of the fathers. Memories of the beautiful Mary were still imprinted in their minds, their jealousy of Albert and the happiness she had brought him, then she had to choose a bloody Irishman ... Why? they asked themselves. As Mary passed Rose's room she heard sobs coming from within. The door was ajar so she peeped in. There was Rose lying on her bed sobbing. "What is wrong, my darling Rose?" she asked. "Oh mother, it is Brendon, he has remembered me. Two years have passed and he still remembers me." Mary went and sat on the bed and put her arms around her daughter. Was this history repeating itself? How many times had she asked herself this question? "Is that why you haven't been dating, Rose, were you waiting for this letter to arrive?" "Mother, I have never forgotten him, the warmth I felt when in his arms, I have never felt this with anyone else. He is so funny, he makes me happy," she told her mother. "Then you must go to him, your heart is sending you a message. I have been there, my darling. You must follow your heart, it is what brings you happiness, nothing else."

First thing for Rose to do today was to post her letter. She spent most of the night writing and rewriting until finally she was happy. She wished it would reach Brendon today, but that was not possible. Perhaps it would take a week to get there and a week for an answer to come back. She was so happy as now she realised why she wasn't interested in other lads. It was Brendon she liked. She found the local lads pompous, just like Charles, that was not what she wanted. She was relieved when her parents told her Charles was in fact her half-brother, but how could her mother have such an arrogant son? She couldn't remember much about her stepfather as she was only four when he died. Mary had not told Rose of the bank account from the estate which would protect her against Charles.

Mail went back and forth between Rose and Brendon, both eager for a reply as soon as the letters were posted. She had long school holidays coming up soon, so she was going to Ireland to stay with her Uncle Patrick and his family. Brendon couldn't wait to see Rose — it was a case of who was the happiest.

The day had arrived when Rose arrived in Ireland. Her uncle picked her up from the station and drove her to his home. The little ones were happy to see their pretty cousin and she was a schoolteacher as well. Patrick had invited Brendon to come for supper that night unbeknown to Rose, as they had arranged to meet the next day. Rose unpacked and tidied herself not for a moment thinking there was going to be a visitor for supper. As the table was being set there was a knock on the door so Patrick asked Rose to answer it. When she opened the door, there stood Brendon. She was everything he had remembered and dreamed of. Her beautiful red Irish hair fell softly down around her shoulders; he wanted to hold her in his arms. Rose stood for a moment then went to him. Before either said a word, they were in each other's arms, it was as if it was only yesterday that they had last seen each other ... not two years! Rose felt safe in his arms, she felt she had come home, a home she had been dreaming of for a very long time. Now she knew where she belonged. It wasn't in Oxshott on the estate, it was here, in Brendon's arms. All through supper their eyes never left each other. Rose was so happy, she wanted supper to be over so she could be alone with him. She wanted him to herself, to talk about all the letters that had gone back and forth and the expressing of feelings between them.

Rose helped with the cleaning up, then she and Brendon went outside together. He took her hand and they walked to the nearest gate which he opened for them to enter the field of wheat. He spread his jacket on the ground so Rose could sit down. They cuddled up together, to just hold each other was all that was needed at this moment. Brendon told her all about his family. He had three sisters who were all working, his mother had passed away and his father lived in a cottage in town. He told Rose that he now knew that his landlord was a lady and that she was Irish and looked after the Irish tenant farmers as she was passionate about the Irish. "How do you know all this?" asked Rose. "Your uncle told me so. He has the same landlord, isn't that strange? Fancy that!" Rose couldn't stop herself laughing. How long was this going to stay a secret? "I love seeing you laugh, Rose, it makes me happy." Poor Brendon, if only he knew what made her laugh, but that could wait, there were more pressing things to attend to right now. She put her arms around him and their lips met, leading them to lie down among the wheat. Rose could feel Brendon's warm body against hers, this she had dreamed of, then she felt his hands on the outside of her dress moving towards her breasts,. She lay back allowing him to gently caress her. He had not meant to move so fast with his feelings, but he found it hard to restrain himself when he was in Rose's arms. No other girl he had dated brought these feelings of wanting. He wanted her body right there and then, but not tonight it would be wrong ... his self-respect was something that was important to him. She was a beautiful young lady and deserved to be treated as such, so his manly wants for her would have to wait a little longer.

His hands lingered on her breasts; this was the first time Rose had let a young man physically touch her body. Others had tried but she told them no! She felt comfortable letting Brendon touch her outside her clothing, as she wanted it to happen as much as he did; it was natural for this to happen between two people who were entering into a relationship. They lay in each other's arms and talked about their lives, but Rose hadn't revealed the full truth to Brendon about her family. That could wait. It was time to go back to the family, so they stood up while Brendon brushed the wheat grass off Rose. He tapped her bottom playfully and Rose responded by reaching up and kissing him. He then knew he hadn't offended her with his forward behaviour. They walked back hand in hand. A message had been given out tonight from one to the other, that this was heading in a direction that was acceptable to both parties. After saying his thank you and goodbyes, Brendon took his leave but not before arranging to pick Rose up tomorrow afternoon.

The next morning Rose had a good discussion with Patrick about teaching in Dunmanway. Was there an opening for teachers? He was sure there was, as the area had suffered badly in the famine and it was only starting to pick up again, but he would make inquiries. Rose told him if the relationship went well then this would be a possibility. All the time the three little children wouldn't leave Rose alone. They took her for a walk around the farm showing her their pigs, a couple of sheep and the horses, all the time telling her they loved living on the farm. The main crop was wheat, but there was always a paddock with potatoes, which was still their staple diet. Rose sat and told Patrick about the situation at home with Charles, that he was arrogant and cold-blooded and how he had gone behind his mother's back to get the title of Lord. This gave him the right to vote with the gentry, which would be against Mary's wishes. But Mary had said as long as she was in charge of the estate, she would not increase the tariffs, but she was waiting to hear if she lost her rights once Charles turned twenty-one. By this time the family in Ireland knew that Joseph was Connor's son.

Rose had changed into a nice dress and brushed her lovely hair as Brendon was due any minute; she was excited to be spending the afternoon with him. They would have supper at the pub so it would probably be later when they returned back. She sat on the wooden bench outside the front door to wait for him. "There he is, there's Brendon," yelled the children as they saw the horse and cart making its way up the driveway. Her heart began to race and he wasn't even near her. He pulled up and jumped down and the children ran to him clinging to his legs. He lifted them high in the air one at a time making them laugh, they thought he was fun; he was good with the little ones. He went over to Rose, "Kiss her, Brendon," they yelled. He did exactly as he was told and he took her in his arms and kissed her. They clapped and laughed. With that he helped Rose up onto the front seat so she could sit beside him while he drove the cart. "You look lovely, Rose, is this special for me?" he teased her. Rose blushed and looked at him, he had a cheeky likeable face. He was of solid build, his arms were muscly and strong, probably because of the farm work, thought Rose. He was just himself and he seemed happy with that, it came out in his personality, he was fun to be around. "I thought we would drive around town so I could show you more of the area, then would you like to come and see where I toil, where I build up these muscles?" he asked as he flexed them showing off to Rose. She couldn't stop smiling. He was always making her laugh; she loved being in his company. As they drove around Brendon pointed out things of interest and people kept calling out to him, he was certainly well known. They headed out of town a couple of miles towards a signpost saying Drinagh; this was where Brendon farmed. The land looked like it was coated in gold as the wheat crops were nearly ready to harvest. Rose had never seen this before and felt it was welcoming her ... such a warm colour!

They approached a property with an entranceway flanked by two fancy gates. "Welcome to my patch of paradise," he said and he leaned over and kissed Rose on the cheek. "Those gates, Brendon, where did they come from? I love them," said Rose. "That is some of my handiwork, I made them. I muck around with scrap metal and turn them into works of art." Rose was taken by surprise; she didn't for a moment think this man of the land was so creative. But as they neared the cottage she could see art work everywhere, he certainly was arty. Outside the cottage door were two love seats painted white, beckoning to be sat on. "These are lovely. Did you make them?" she asked. "Yes, more of my handiwork." He helped her down and she walked over and sat in one of the seats. Brendon was full of surprises. He took her hand and led her inside. There hanging from the walls and ceiling were fancy hooks with all the kitchen utensils. Rose was amazed, it felt so homely and inviting. Although the cottage was very small, his handiwork was everywhere.

He led her to his bedroom where a beautiful iron bedhead stood with its gold-painted finials. "This is beautiful, Brendon. Did you make it?" "Yes," he said proudly. What a talented lad, thought Rose. She felt so proud of him. Who would have expected this from this hearty soul? They went outside and sat in a love seat together. The scene before them was amazing, the colour gold was everywhere and it radiated a feeling of warmth. Brendon put his arms around Rose and leaned over and kissed her. She nestled into him feeling the warmth from his body. "Do you like it here?" she asked. "This was my family home, my father's farm. Now it is mine; it is all I know Rose, it is my life. I would like more acres but because I am only a tenant farmer I can ask for no more. A family can survive here with little or no extras. That is why I make things, so I can sell them and make extra income. I never want to be poor. One day I would like to have a wife and family so I want to provide well for them." "You deserve to get on, Brendon, and I hope you find what you are looking for," said Rose. He wanted to tell her he had found what he wanted, she was right here with him. He did wonder what her life was like; all he knew was that she was a schoolteacher, and he had met her parents. She dressed beautifully and spoke well, but that would be because she had a teaching position. He hadn't met anyone educated before so he tried hard to show he would be worthy of her; this worried him a little. Rose reached over and put her arms around him. Brendon took this as an invite to express his feelings. He stood up and took her hand and led her inside to his bedroom. They sat down on the bed and began to kiss passionately, then Brendon eased her down so they lay together with their bodies touching. He moved his hands over her body bringing them up to caress her breasts. Rose enjoyed Brendon touching her; his hands were gentle and his kisses were hot and passionate making her cling to him, pulling his body into hers. She had never felt these feelings before and was excited as to what was going to happen next. Brendon moved his hands inside of Rose's dress and touched her bare skin caressing her body, then he untied her bodice and cupped her bare breasts in his hands. They felt warm and soft and as he caressed her he could feel her body arching full of desire, which was all the encouragement he needed. "Are you sure this is what you want from me, Rose?" he asked. "Let us just touch each other and take it from there," he whispered. He undid his shirt and took her hands guiding them to his muscly chest. He slipped his hands down her back onto her buttocks, touching her, arousing her. Her body welled with love, she wanted him to take her, but she was frightened of the consequences, so let him know. He sensed she wasn't fully committed so they enjoyed the touching and the feelings they were experiencing. Rose remembered her mother's dilemma and how she came to be, so she told Brendon this story while she lay in his arms. He understood her concerns and loved her for that. It stopped there.

Now it was time to eat, as they were both hungry; they had worked up an appetite. They drove into town to the little pub where it all began. Brendon ordered them both a drink to have with their supper. He wanted to know more about Rose's life; she hadn't told him much thus far. She looked into his eyes. What would she tell him? Was it time to reveal the truth, as she knew deep down she had fallen in love with him. She would wait until they finished eating. Brendon joked with her making her laugh, he was so funny and the teasing never stopped. When they finished dining they went to the bar which was packed, so they stood together waiting until a seat became available. While Brendon went to get them another drink, a young man came up to Rose and asked her to dance. She declined but he grabbed her hand and led her to where people were dancing and proceeded to take her in his arms. Rose looked around for Brendon but could not see him. It didn't take long for him to find her. "What are you doing dancing with my girl, Sean?" he asked the guy. "You lucky beggar, where did you find such a beauty, Brendon?" "Never you mind there, Sean, Rose is my girl." Sean thanked Rose and off he went. "Oh, so I am your girl now?" teased Rose. With this he kissed her. "You are all mine, Rose, I will not share you with anyone." This is possession talk, she thought, and felt proud that he lay claim to her. They managed to find a seat in a quiet corner. Brendon looked at her and knew deep down how he felt about her; she was his girl. Rose was still not ready to tell him that her family were the absentee owners of his and many other farms, as she wasn't sure how he would react to this. She wanted to make sure he loved her for herself, not like the young men back at the estate; to them she was the prize trophy. They danced together and joined in the singing, in all having a great time. This is what Rose loved about the Irish; there was no talk of money simply because no-one had much, it was all about fun and laughter. She kept thinking back to her mother's story and her overwhelming love for her father.

The next morning Patrick and his family were going to church. "Will you come with us, Rose?" he asked. "Please, please, Rose, come with us?" pleaded the children. With this they all set off for church, and the children argued as to who was going to sit next to Rose on the cart. They sang as they trotted along the gravel road, their teeth chattering because of the corrugation. This was rural Ireland at its best. The little church was filled with the locals and everyone seemed to know each other. The children had told their friends at school that their cousin was a schoolteacher in London, and this went around like wildfire. It was very hard to attract teachers to the poorer rural areas.

After the service Rose was approached by a headmaster from a local school as he believed that Rose had thought about a teaching position in Dunmanway. He laughed while speaking to her. "Your young cousins told everyone you were going to marry Brendon and live in the area. I just thought I would get in first," he said. Poor Rose, she felt embarrassed. "Well, that hasn't been established yet, but if it happens I will definitely let you know," she told him. Next, they walked to the churchyard where the headstones were. Rose went and sat by Joseph's headstone and cried, remembering him as her best friend when growing up together. Joseph was always talked about by the family but the way he died was taboo. She said a little prayer for Joseph and hugged his headstone. On the way back to the farm Rose asked who had told the headmaster that she and Brendon were going to get married. "We did, because we saw you kissing," they yelled. "You ratbags, you didn't say that, did you?" asked Patrick and he apologised to Rose, thus bringing laughter from all.

It was nearly time for Rose to return to Oxshott and her teaching job. She was spending her last day with Brendon and she asked him to take her to the church so she could say goodbye to Joseph and leave flowers by his headstone. As they stood together by the headstone, he noticed that Joseph's surname was Irish, not English like Rose's, yet they were siblings. "Rose, why is your brother's surname not the same as yours?" he asked. This brought tears to her eyes. How was she going to explain it to Brendon? It was so complicated; it was a story of true love and passion. Would he understand? She didn't know where to start. "I told you what happened to Joseph, and that we all think it was Charles who fired the gun, not Joseph." Then the tears started. "Father's heart was broken. Deep down we know he blames Charles." "That is really sad, Rose," said Brendon, then all else was forgotten.

"Let's go home to your cottage and spend the rest of the day there. We'll buy a bite of lunch and take it with us," suggested Rose. "We will not buy lunch, I will cook lunch for you, don't go arranging things," he told her sternly. Then he laughed as he hoped she wanted to spend the day with him on his own. They drove the cart out to Brendon's. It was a bit chilly today, so he put his jacket around her shoulders. "But you will get cold, Brendon," said Rose. "What, with muscles like these?" and he flexed them. "I am never cold, besides now I have your love to keep me warm." Rose blushed with this statement. As they entered the cottage there were hot embers glowing in the fireplace so Brendon put a log on the fire. It wasn't long before the fire started to roar. He put the kettle on the stove and lay a tablecloth on the wooden table, then brought out some fresh bread he had baked that morning. He sizzled some home-grown bacon in a pan, then put it on the table to have with the bread. Rose was amazed with what he had whipped up in a short time. This was the Irish, they were so resourceful, the men included; imagine the gentry lads making bread and cooking bacon ... that's what their mothers were for!

After lunch they walked around the farm, with Brendon

telling Rose about his dream of owning a farm of his own one day, but that it was an impossible dream, but he would hang on to it even if it was just in his mind. Rose asked if the farm next door was tenanted and yes, it was, but not by the same landlord as his. Most of the other farms in the area were owned by the Rothchilds, the largest landowners. "Is your surname spelt the same as theirs?" ask Brendon. "Yes, I think so," replied Rose. "I am thankful we can make an average living, not one you would be accustomed to, I wouldn't think, but us Irish people of the land, we were born to work for the English gentry. It was not so once. Our lands were taken off us by the then King of England and given to his knights and followers. Now instead of owning our lands we are just caretakers of our own lands. It doesn't seem fair, Rose, but this is our lot whether we like it or not. I am thankful for my life; one must find the positives in everything and turn it into happiness.

"You know, Brendon, you are the first person I have met who can find happiness from so little and still be thankful. That is a wonderful quality for anyone to have," said Rose lovingly. "That's why you are attracted to me, Rose," he said with a cheeky grin. That grin said it all. Rose knew in her heart this was the man she was meant to find. She put her arms around him. This was her man. Her heart was beating fast. "Please, take me home, Brendon?" she asked. They walked back hand in hand and upon reaching the cottage Rose led him into his bedroom. She undressed from her waist up and stood in front of him. He just stood and stared at her body, she was beautiful, then he reached out and drew her closer towards him. He bent down and kissed her neck, then moved down her body. Rose stood and took all these feelings in; this she had never done before, she had saved herself for this moment with Brendon. He lay her on his bed and then undressed. Rose reached out to touch him and ran her hands over his muscles and down his chest; he was such a strongly built guy. Then her hands lingered around his manly parts, playfully touching them. "Are you sure you want to give yourself to me, Rose? This will cement our love for each other whatever the consequences," he confirmed. "Please take me, Brendon," she whispered. Their bodies came together; he knew this was her first time to be bedded so he was gentle with her, until she begged him for more. Then passion took over and Brendon's bed was tested to the limit. They lay in each other's arms afterwards, not a word was spoken. They both knew what this meant, it was a binding commitment to each other. The cottage was warm and they both drifted off to sleep. It was late afternoon when they stirred and Rose laughed as she looked at Brendon. "Am I that funny?" he asked. "I was thinking, just as well you built a sturdy bed." "I knew one day it would be put to good use," he joked back. This was good old Irish banter. "I'm going to miss you, Rose. Promise me you will come back next school break. You are my girl, I will stay true to you, my darling," he promised. "Brendon, to me today said it all. I have saved myself for someone special and you are that someone. I have fallen in love with you. You have the most wonderful outlook on life and I love being in your company, you make me so happy. I will come back next break and we will make arrangements for our future. "Thank you, Rose, you are my soulmate. There are still lots of things I don't know about you but next time you can tell me."

"We had better get you back before it gets too dark," he said, and off they set. When they reached the uncle's place,

Brendon jumped down and helped Rose alight. They stood holding on to each other, neither wanting to let go. "Goodbye, my darling Rose, don't forget about me and my strong bed," he reminded her. "I will never forget what happened in your bed, Brendon, it was so special." With this they said their goodbyes.

The next morning Patrick took Rose to the train station, then she caught the ferry and the train back to Oxshott and a carriage home. She couldn't wait to tell her family how she felt about Brendon, and the thought of shifting to Ireland to live. She loved Ireland and especially the Irish people. They were so far removed from the stuffy English gentry; wealth was never talked about, it wasn't important, that was because most people were very poor. Her family welcomed her home and wanted to know how it all went with Brendon. She told them everything ... well, most things! They were happy for her. "Is Charles not home?" she asked. "He will be in his room," said Connor. When they sat down to supper he arrived at the table. He asked Rose what she thought of Ireland. "I loved it, I met a nice guy there, I am thinking of applying for a teaching position in Dunmanway," she replied. "Poor you, how could anyone live with the Irish? They live in poverty," he stated. "That is because the gentry keep putting up the land tariffs," said an irate Rose. "And rightly so, we need their money for our lifestyles." "Would you do that knowing you have uncles on tenant farms?" "Too right I would. We talked about this at college, the Irish are there to work for us," said a pompous Charles. "You are heartless, Charles," sobbed Rose. "No, I am a lord, a businessman, our land must make us money." With this Connor got up and left the table, he had heard enough. "Charles, I think you need to think about Connor's and my heritage, we are both

Irish. That was insensitive what you have just said, in fact it was hurting," stated Mary. "Get used to it, mother, you live in England now. Father was a rich landlord, you owe this lifestyle to him." "I loved your father, he took me in, but if he was here today he would not be proud to hear you talk like this. After I explained to him how the Irish suffered he was sympathetic and voted against raising the tariffs. When I took over I told the gentry to do what they liked but I would not increase them." "As a lord, mother, when it is my turn to vote, I will go with the gentry," confirmed Charles. Rose looked across at her mother and saw the hurt in her eyes. Nothing more was discussed. Charles had had his big ego boost; no-one was impressed with his non-sentimental values towards his parent's heritage.

"So, you are thinking of going to Ireland, Rose. You must think a lot of Brendon?" asked Mary. "Yes, mother, he has such happiness in his heart, not like the lads around here. All they can talk about is money and themselves. He loves the farm life, he doesn't know we are his landlords, I haven't told him yet," said Rose. "So, he is just a tenant farmer then, and to think he works his butt off for us?" quipped Charles. "Yes, Charles, he is only a tenant farmer but he knows of happiness and is very thankful for his life," fired back Rose. "That proves how backward the Irish are, fancy being happy being a tenant farmer." "You are the only pompous aristocrat in this family, Charles. You don't know happiness, you are only interested in yourself and your wealth, but one day you will regret how you treated your family, mark my words!" went out a warning from his sister.

There were only two days before Charles went back to college; the sooner the better for everyone. Connor kept well out of his way; he was disgusted with Charles' behaviour towards his family. The title of 'Lord' had certainly gone to his head but Mary would not let it be used on the estate. He was Lord Charles to everyone outside the gates. Today Rose had decided to go to town to post a letter to Brendon and on the way home she was stopped by a couple of the local lads inviting her to a party at the weekend. "Thank you but no, I already have a boyfriend," she told them. "Who is the lucky fellow?" they wanted to know. "He is an Irishman and his name is Brendon." Why were the Irishmen winning all the prize trophies? They knew of her mother's preference for the Irish, as it had been common knowledge among the gentry for years.

As she was entering the gates to the estate she saw Charles standing on the edge of the woods with a gun in his hand. When he saw her, he pointed the gun in the air and fired. That was the last thing she remembered. Connor was in the stables attending the horses when he saw Rose's carriage in the yard. He thought that was unusual as she always tethered them when she came home. He continued working away until he heard Mary calling him. "Connor, the twins heard a shot and wondered where it came from. Did you hear anything?" He ran to the tool-shed only to find the gun gone. "Charles must have the gun," he said. "Is Rose in the home?" he asked. Mary said that she hadn't arrived home yet. It was then the alarm bells started ringing. Why was her horse and carriage in the yard? The twins ran down the driveway to where the shot had come from and found Rose lying on the road. They tried to wake her but she wouldn't talk to them, so one ran back towards the home and one stayed with her. "Mother, father, it's Rose, she's hurt!" he called.

They both came running to where she lay. Connor tried to wake her but she was unconscious. He ran back to fetch the carriage. Mary was in tears as were the twins. Just as they were lifting her into the carriage, out of the woods strolled Charles with the gun in his arm. "What's all the commotion about?" he asked. "Did you fire the gun about ten minutes ago?" yelled Connor. "Yes, I shot at a fox," he answered. Connor was furious, he couldn't bring himself to say any more to Charles. "Rose fell from the carriage; the horse must have reared when you fired. She is unconscious, we are taking her to the hospital," Mary told him. He shrugged his shoulders. "I hope she is okay," then off he walked.

The twins wanted to come to the hospital but there wasn't enough room as they had to lay Rose across the seat. They drove to the hospital and Rose was stretchered in, Connor and Mary explained what had happened, then they were shown to a waiting room. Mary couldn't stop crying. This was their first-born, she didn't want to lose her; they had lost Joseph, surely not Rose as well. Connor held her hand, he was in shock ... the cause of all this: Charles!

The doctor came and spoke to them to say she was still unconscious and that they would have to wait, so told them to go home and come back in the morning. Connor didn't want to leave Rose, but Mary said he would be needed at home for the twins. They left the hospital and drove home. Connor was distancing himself more and more from Charles; he had tried to be a good father to him. But as he grew older and learnt that his father was a lord and that the estate belonged to his family, he felt he had ownership to it above his mother. He had heard through the gentry that his father had fallen in love with an Irish beauty but by family tradition and birthright the estate should pass on to him. Connor knew deep down that Charles would challenge his mother when he became of age.

Was this accident with Rose another way to open the door for him to gain a larger share of the estate? He was frightened what was going to happen next, he did not trust Charles. While driving home he mentioned this to Mary. "I am worried about Charles, Mary, where is this going? Is he out to get the estate at any cost? I don't feel safe here with our family." "You are right, Connor, I am worried too. He goes back to college tomorrow, then we can discuss this. Let us worry about our darling Rose." The twins were happy to have their parents back home as they were frightened being left with Charles. They wanted to know how Rose was. Mary hugged them and said there would be no news until tomorrow. "Where is Charles?" she asked. "He took the horse and cart to a friend's place, he didn't even stay to see how Rose was. Why is he so horrible?" they asked. Mary made some supper for them and they sat and talked about Rose going to live in Ireland. This was a big shock to them all, as they loved her and would miss her dearly. No-one wanted her to leave, she was a big part of their family. Of course, the twins didn't know that Rose was their blood sister, as her surname was Rothchild and theirs was O'Leary, but when the time was right they would be told.

The next morning Charles was leaving for college so Mary told him to be ready early as they wanted to go to the hospital; they would drop him off at the train station on their way. He performed, as he didn't want to have to wait at the station. "For once, Charles, this is not about you. You will do as you are told, you will be dropped off at the station. Your sister is lying in hospital, she is the important one at the moment," said an angry Mary. Charles didn't answer, he was sulking.

The twins sat up front with their father, so this just left Mary and Charles in the carriage. "Your father was very dear to me, Charles. You are not like him. He was a caring man, you are so selfish. Why?" asked Mary. "I want this estate, it belongs to me as his eldest son, I am entitled to it," he replied. "No, Charles, you have no rights until you are twenty-one." "All you care about are the Irish because that is your heritage. What about my English heritage?" he asked. "Don't forget you have Irish blood as well as English," Mary reminded him. He hated hearing this, true as it was. "When I become a qualified estate lawyer I will know the laws of peerage and what I am entitled to. Rose shouldn't be entitled to anything, she is just a daughter, it is the sons who have rights." "Yes, but if Joseph was still here he would have inherited the lordship and part of the estate; you as the second son would not have been entitled to it," Mary let him know. "He's not here, so it's mine, that's all that matters," said a selfish Charles. Mary was thankful Connor had not heard this conversation; he would surely have hit Charles, as he missed Joseph so much. As much as Mary tried to keep her position as mother to Charles, she could see it slipping away. He wanted the estate and peerage at any cost! She could see she would have to make some decisions to protect certain people before he turned twenty-one.

"Right, we are here," yelled Connor as he pulled up at the train station. Charles and Mary climbed out. As Mary went to hug him he walked away without so much as a goodbye to anyone. "Next time you come home, bring some manners with you, young man," Connor called to him. Charles just kept walking.

Next it was on to the hospital as everyone, except Charles, was concerned about Rose. She had regained consciousness but they still had tests to do. She smiled at them but was still in terrible pain. They gathered around her bed. Connor took her hand, remembering at that moment how she came to be. He loved this girl so much, and tears ran down his face, as he thought back to that day when he met the beautiful Irish lass without a name. Rose was very quiet, she was missing Brendon. How she wished he was here with her. They had only said goodbye to each other a few days ago and already she was pining for him. She asked Mary to let the school know that she was in hospital as she was due to start back the day after tomorrow, so they would have to find a replacement teacher. Amid all the chatter Rose drifted off to sleep. The nurse asked them to leave so they could do more tests on her, and hopefully by tonight they would know more. Everyone was relieved that Charles was gone for another term; he would not be missed.

On returning to the hospital that night they were met by the doctor. He told them Rose would be in hospital for at least three weeks as she had fractured her back, so she needed complete bed rest. She was devastated when they walked in. "I won't be able to teach for at least six weeks, the doctor has just told me," she said amid her tears. "We want you to get better, don't worry about the teaching," Connor told her as he bent down and kissed his daughter. Rose was feeling down. "I miss Brendon, I wish he was here with me," she sobbed. They tried to cheer her up and take her mind away from Brendon. "Where is Charles? He hasn't been to see me, but then he wouldn't, would he?" she said. Mary couldn't understand why she would say that, so she asked Rose. She told them she remembered seeing Charles by the woods with the gun and when he saw her he fired the gun in the air. That was all she remembered. Connor looked at Mary. So that is what happened — the gunshot caused the horse to rear up, and it was done deliberately. But he said he was shooting at a fox! "Charles has gone back to college, that is the best place for him," explained Connor.

As they were driving home, the twins asked if perhaps they wrote to Brendon and asked him to come and stay, that would make Rose happy. Connor thought that was a great idea, but Mary remembered that Rose hadn't told him anything about her background. Would it frighten him off if he knew the wealth surrounding Rose? Perhaps he wouldn't feel worthy of her, being a tenant farmer. She would think about it over the next couple of days. The following day Rose was feeling much better; she had got over the initial shock, but she still mentioned she was missing Brendon.

Two weeks had passed and Connor was off to the train station to pick up Brendon. This was going to be a total shock to him but Mary was prepared. First thing he wanted to know was his Rose going to be okay, and what had happened to her. Connor explained everything, and Brendon thought back to what Rose had told him what had happened to Joseph. Was this that same Charles?

As they pulled into the estate Brendon couldn't believe what he saw before him. "Good God, man, is this where Rose lives?" he asked in shock. He didn't receive an answer from Connor, as this was up to Mary to explain. "Hello, Brendon, Rose is going to be so happy to see you as she is missing you. We haven't told her you are coming so she will be surprised." Brendon just stood unable to speak. Surely this wasn't Rose's home; suddenly he felt inadequate when he thought back to his little cottage in Ireland. He had never seen such grandeur. Who were these people? He knew Rose's surname was Rothchild but he never associated her with this sort of wealth. What had she thought of his little piece of farm that he was so proud of, when she was part of this estate? Mary could see how uncomfortable he felt. "Come, Brendon, we will have a cup of tea. The twins are waiting to meet you," said Mary as she invited him into the drawing room. He was still in denial that this was Rose's life, she seemed so sweet and natural ... but this! The twins were introduced to Brendon and he shook their hands. "Pleased to meet you, young men. Do you live in all this grandeur? I am still in shock," was all he could get out. The boys laughed. "We are just ordinary people, we don't think of our life being any different to anyone else," they said. This put him at ease, just a little. Mary decided it was time to explain, so she told him this was their estate, and yes, it was Rose's home. She hadn't told him as she didn't think it was relevant; when two people met and fell in love, nothing else mattered. "Rose was frightened of losing you if you knew her background. She loves you, Brendon, for who you are, you make her happy, that is all that matters to her. Don't let any of this come between the two of you, it is irrelevant to happiness, and that is what you bring her," Mary told him with all sincerity. It was not the time to mention anything else. He had a lot to absorb at this moment; she didn't want to overload him. "You will have to excuse me, I can't believe all this. Rose seemed so ordinary and natural although I noticed she spoke very clear English. I wonder now what she thought of me, just a tenant farmer, one who was proud of what he had, even though my land is owned by the English gentry. Now that I think of it, my landowner has the same name as you people, Rothchild ..." Before he could continue, Mary interrupted. "You may as well hear it all, Brendon, now that we have come this far. We are the Rothchilds, the absentee English landowners. "So, you are the Irish lass that has looked after us tenant farmers, good God, well I never," said a gobsmacked Brendon. Everyone laughed at his remark, he was such a humble being, a true Irishman. No wonder Rose was drawn to him; he reminded her of her Irish lover!

At the hospital Mary and Connor walked in and greeted Rose. She was a little down today, but they knew it wouldn't be for long. They both kissed her, then Mary picked up her hairbrush and brushed her beautiful hair. It shone like gold; she always remembered Albert telling her this, and it made her feel special. Then the big surprise: in walked Brendon and the twins. Rose burst into tears; she had been thinking about him all night wishing he was here with her. "Hi, my darling Rose, I hope you are being looked after all right?" he asked as he bent down and kissed her. He sat on the bed holding her hand. "Oh Brendon, I have missed you, you will never know how much," Rose said. "Yes, I do, because I have missed you just as much," he replied. "I guess you know all about my life, without me telling you. Don't be afraid, Brendon, superficial things are just that, they don't come from the heart, they are there to see, they have no feelings." "But, Rose, my humble life and place, they are not what you are used to. I felt proud sharing my life with you, but we live in different worlds," he said. "Feelings have nothing to do with wealth or poverty, they come from the heart, whether rich or poor. Feelings don't differentiate, they are not governed by a person's position in life. You make me laugh, you bring happiness to my life; nothing else matters. I love your little cottage, it has you stamped all over it. Everywhere I looked I saw things you had made, not bought, made with your own hands. That is so special, Brendon," Rose told him. Her family witnessed this conversation and there wasn't a dry eye among them. Here were two people telling each other how they felt and that feelings were more important than anything that surrounded them. Connor held Mary's hand — this was their story all over again! "Come, boys, let these two have a little time together," said Connor, and with this they left.

The boys told their parents they liked Brendon and they knew he would look after Rose. "What a pity we all couldn't live in Ireland," they said. "But you were only young when we took Joseph back, it is so different to your life here," said Mary. "But, mother, everyone teases us about our red Irish hair. If we lived in Ireland, we wouldn't look any different to anyone else. Besides, as Rose said, wealth doesn't bring happiness. She loves Brendon's little cottage perhaps more than our big home." Mary and Connor could not believe what they had just heard; they thought the boys were happy living in the luxury that surrounded them. "You mean you would leave all we have here, to live in Ireland with less?" asked Mary. "Mother, we are a family. We don't want to lose Rose, we love her." "What about Charles?" asked Mary. "He doesn't care about us, he didn't even care about Rose, we hate him for what he did to her, imagine if we lost her too? He thinks he is better than us, he doesn't need us but we need each other." Their parents were stunned by this revelation. They thought the estate was all the happiness the family needed, now it appeared it was not! "Rose told us the people are very friendly. It is not so here, for us, as the gentry children think they are better than us, we are just ordinary kids." Mary and Connor had not heard the twins expressing how they felt about life, but here it was told from their hearts. It was time to go back and say their goodbyes to Rose. Brendon could have her to himself tomorrow.

Today Brendon had gone to spend the day with Rose at the hospital. Mary had turned a lot of things over in her head. "Connor, I want you to hide the gun from Charles so he can't find it. He cannot be trusted," she said. The twins had expressed their concern about Charles and why Rose was in hospital. They were of the opinion that he was going to put them off the estate once he was twenty-one. "Well, we might just make it hard for him," said Mary with anger in her voice. Connor didn't join in the conversation, he was shocked when he heard what had caused Rose's accident. This confirmed his thoughts on Charles; he was one to watch. Did he lose his other son because of his desire to become a lord? Tears welled in his eyes. Mary noticed these and knew exactly why they were there, and whom they were for.

How were they going to deal with Charles? What would he try next? Were any of them safe? Now that Mary knew the estate did not mean so much to the twins, and with Rose shifting to Ireland, did any of them need to be there? All the joy the estate had brought was now fading due to one person. Once Charles came home aged twenty-one as a qualified estate lawyer, he as the lord would rule the roost. Mary discussed with Connor what she would like to happen, so she made an appointment with the solicitor, as she didn't fully understand her position with the estate and where she stood with Charles.

Mary told her solicitor what had happened with Charles and Rose. He was very helpful and advised Mary of her rights. She wanted to know if she could take land out of the estate. Providing it wasn't more than her share and if Rose was in agreeance, then they had the rights to Mary's half and Rose's quarter share. He wanted to know about the English estate. What did she propose to do with it, because it was dependent on income from the Irish lands. Mary said Charles could have it, and if the land that was left was not enough to keep the estate going, then he was just going to have to subsidise with money from other means. She didn't want it to be easy for him, as he clearly thought by rights it was his. His position as Lord Charles Rothchild was going to be somewhat diminished when he found his land was going to be reduced, but he still had a good holding as his father's holdings were substantial indeed. Mary would work out what land she wanted then come back and they could get it under way, as there was some urgency with it. Time was ticking to Charles's twenty-first.

Rose was back home but not allowed to start teaching for another two weeks. Brendon had gone back to Ireland as he could only leave the farm for six days. Mary and Connor spoke with her about her share of the estate and she was in agreeance that it be taken out. Mary told Rose that Brendon's farm would become her share and they would own it outright. Rose was reduced to tears; all Brendon ever wanted was to own his own farm and now it was a reality, but nothing was to be said until everything was finalised with the solicitor. Mary wanted to look after her brothers and their farms. Connor suggested they still collect the land tariffs, but those payments would go towards paying off their own farms, which they would ultimately own. Mary thought this was an excellent way of helping them, and if in the future she wanted to gift them the land, they would feel they had contributed towards owning their farms.

But what of Mary, Connor and the twins' future? Connor had never mentioned to Mary what his future dreams held. He was the mainstay that held the family together; he was grateful for the life Mary had afforded him. But now it was his time to let her know what he wanted for himself. The twins loved the land and so did he. He had always fancied having a large workshop where he could charge to fix equipment for other people, to make a living and feel he could contribute to supporting his family. "If we kept a couple of farms that the twins and I could work together and combine with my workshop, I would be really happy," he told Mary. "I didn't realise I had a dream until now. Let us make a complete new life for ourselves in our homeland away from all this pomp and ceremony. Let Charles have it, I'm not happy here any longer, I'm frightened for my family. Let us be near our Joseph again?" Mary was in tears hearing this from her lover. She had never asked him what he wanted from life. He was always there when she needed him, and she had just presumed he was happy, but now he wanted to provide for her and their family.

Mary and her lawyer worked together on taking the farms out of the estate, the ones she wanted to keep for her family and her siblings. Rose was to get Brendon's farm as her share. Mary had regained the ownership of ten farms leaving Charles with eight, which if he lived a less extravagant life would provide the costs of running the estate. This was going to be told to him once he turned twenty-one, and by then Mary and Connor would have other plans in place. The twins were happy with the thought of moving to Ireland. Once the legal titles were signed to Mary, it was up to her what she did with her lands.

12

Charles's Reign

It was now approaching Charles's twenty-first birthday. Because he was a brilliant scholar he had completed and passed his papers so was now a qualified estate lawyer. Mary had asked him what he wanted to do for his 21st birthday. Charles being Charles, he wanted an elaborate party held on the estate and he wanted special cooks to supply and handle the food; this he would arrange himself. Mary, Connor and the twins had been to Ireland and sorted out a farm they liked at Curraghnaloughra, one they would like to live on. They picked out a house plan and sorted out builders that could start building straight away, as once Charles was told of his reduced land holdings, they didn't know the consequences for the family. This was also going to affect the gentry as they relied on all of Mary's lands to pull weight with the relevant authorities. She was going to be one unpopular lady. She would manage her farms from Ireland and that would be where her wheat would stay; it would not be imported across the Irish Sea, it would be sold to the people of Ireland.

Rose was now in Ireland teaching at a Dunmanway school. She and Brendon were engaged; they hadn't set a wedding date as they were waiting until her family shifted to Ireland. She didn't want to invite Charles to her wedding as she had so many bad memories of him. It would just be a family affair and close friends. She had broken her ties with England, much to the disappointment the Oxshott gentry community; they were hoping one of their own would snare Rose Rothchild ... instead it was a bloody Irishman.

Now that Charles was living back at home, he had grown up a bit, but he had not lost his pompous attitude. He had taken his position as lord very seriously thus thinking he was an important person, but he soon learnt that on the estate and among his family, he was just one of them. He had acquired an office in town and started his own legal firm; above the entrance to his office was a sign 'Lord Charles Rothchild' that was to inform people he was important, he was a lord. When he became of age he would make changes on the estate, but at the moment he had to tread water ... he couldn't wait! He got on well with the gentry, but of course he was one of them. Mary had been to visit her solicitor to find out if she still had voting power for the estate, but alas, the position of Lord overruled her. Not that it really mattered any more because they would be leaving the estate soon; she was still going to be a wealthy lady. The profit from the Irish lands over the past years had put a large amount, a very large amount into her private account. She didn't know if Charles thought there would be a stash of money in the bank,; if so, he would be in for a big surprise. Rose's bank account was looking good but she hadn't been told of this; it would be a nice wedding present for her and Brendon.

The family only saw Charles when he came home from work although most nights he dined out with the gentry. Connor and he were distancing themselves from each other. Connor was upset because Charles ignored the twins; it was as if they didn't exist. His only real family contact was with Mary and that was only when he felt like it. The twins were bursting with excitement about moving to Ireland but it all had to be kept under wraps. No-one knew of the family's future plans. This would be revealed after Charles turned twenty-one; they would let him have his moment of glory.

Charles had arranged cooks from a local inn to come and have a look at the estate's cooking facilities, for his big day. He wanted everything to be of the best. He had notable college friends coming to stay on the estate, among them lawyers, a doctor, and a couple of lecturers. Because it was in the school holidays he had even remembered to ask Rose, who had to ask if she could bring Brendon as he wasn't invited. She was upset about this and would have refused to come, but she knew her mother would need her support. These days Connor stayed well out of the picture. He was totally over Charles, who had forgotten who had been a father to him since he was a baby. All he wanted to remember was that he was the son of Lord Albert Rothchild, that was all that mattered to him ... a name.

Mary worked on the gardens, they were a credit to her. The twins helped when they could, but they preferred to be in the tool-shed with their father. She was going to miss the beautiful rosebeds and lawns but she would be able to establish her own garden in Curraghnaloughra. Connor loved pottering in the stables and the workshop. Who would look after them? Little did he know Charles was going to hire staff. He was going to employ a groundsman, a butler, and a cook regardless of what Mary and Connor thought. Then he could give orders, and the staff would have to call him Lord Charles. But where was the money going to come from,? His income would be halved!

Only two days to go until the big day. Rose and Brendon had arrived making the household happy again. Rose looked beautiful, she had blossomed into a lovely young lady. The twins got on well with Brendon, he was like a brother to them. They would go into the woods squirrel hunting and looking for foxes. If he wasn't with them he was in the workshop with Connor. He was a real outdoor guy, and a happy one at that, always laughing and joking. Nothing escaped his keen eye for spare metal, he was always on the lookout. Connor looked at him and thought this was the kind of lad he would want Joseph to have been, no wonder Rose loved him. Charles was not impressed. He thought Rose could have done much better; wait until she saw some of his colleagues that were coming to stay, they would think she was a bit of all right. Brendon was only a tenant farmer, what did Rose see in him? He couldn't see that he made her happy and that all the family liked him. He made them laugh with his Irish wit. Rose adored him and was always touching him, which Charles thought was sickening. Brendon had formed his own opinion of Charles; he saw him as a self-righteous cold person, one he disliked from the moment he met him. Charles had all but ignored him, but this didn't worry Brendon, he had better things to do. Charles hoped that one of his upper-class friends would steal Rose away from him, he was a nobody.

Rose helped her mother prepare rooms for Charles's guests. The food was all taken care of by his hired cooks, all the family had to do was pay for everything. It was going to cost, but they knew this was the calm before the storm. They would let Charles bathe in all his glory, before his world was halved.

Mary had spent hours with her solicitor getting the final details in order. Charles had no rights to the past financials of the estate, it was only applicable from the day he turned twenty-one. This was when his reign would begin. Both Mary and her solicitor would arrange a meeting with Charles the week following his coming of age, as this was where he was going to learn his fate, not at the estate where he could turn on everyone. Mary wanted the rest of her family spared, especially Connor, as now Charles looked down on him because he was Irish; he was an embarrassment to him now he had the position of a lord. Other people's feelings meant nothing to Charles, as long as he was okay.

The big day had arrived. Charles was strutting around giving orders, checking that everything was perfect. Everyone was going to see his fabulous estate, and his mother had the gardens looking picture perfect. The local gentry were invited for nibbles and drinks, all the important people of the area would be there. It commenced around two o'clock in the afternoon. Connor and Brendon had escaped to the stables for the morning as there had to be plenty of room for the carriages and horses to be tethered. The twins had been given their orders: one had to be at the entrance to take the guests' coats and hats and then put them on the special racks that Charles had bought. The other had to take the carriage to the train station and pick up guests and bring them back to the estate. The cooks had arrived and were preparing food needed throughout the day and into the night.

Mary and Rose went to prepare themselves for the onslaught of Charles's guests. Mary brushed her hair until it shone like gold; she wanted Charles to be proud of her. She was in her mid-forties and was still a fine-looking lady. Rose was the blossoming flower now, she was a younger vision of her mother. They both looked beautiful as they walked down the stairs, even Charles passed a comment; he must have been in a good mood, thought Rose. The first guests were delivered from the station; they were two of Charles's college friends and were very upper-class. "What a lovely place you have, Lord Charles, the estate looks fabulous, the gardens are outstanding," they commented. Charles greeted them and introduced them to Rose. "Rose will take you to your rooms so you can put your bags down," he said. They were stunned by Lord Charles's sister, she was such a beauty; there would certainly be rivalry among them to win her heart. She explained where to find everything on the estate and told them to feel free to wonder around. They were in awe of Lord Charles's wealth and his beautiful sister. When they came down after settling in, Charles took them for a walk around the estate. Mary was on her way back from the conservatory when she ran into Charles and his friends. "This is my mother, Mary." They greeted her politely and commented on the lovely estate. Beauty certainly ran in the family, what a stunning lady; Lord Charles certainly had it all. As they passed the stables, Charles introduced Connor as his stepfather, then casually introduced Brendon not bothering to mention he was Rose's fiancé.

The men decided it was time to go and change into respectable dress for this posh party. As Connor made his way upstairs he looked out the window and saw Mary in the garden. She looked beautiful, he felt so proud of her. His love for her was as deep now as it was the day he met her and she still made his heart flutter. It would be sad to take her away from her years of work in the gardens, they were so manicured. She would miss them, but soon their life was going to take a new path. Connor knew it was time for them to make a new life for themselves where there would be no reminders of their past life, other than their children. He no longer wanted to be a kept man; he needed to get some self-worth. Not that it mattered as Mary was still a wealthy woman, but it was a sense of worth. Ireland was going to be where they were returning, and it couldn't come soon enough. He had never been accepted by the gentry; he was the Irishman that stole the heart of the woman they all dreamed of bedding. This, he was never forgiven for, but wait for the news that they were shifting and taking over half the estate's tenanted lands ... what then?

Rose was helping Brendon to change but she was more of a hindrance than a help as she kept distracting him. She looked radiant today; he couldn't keep his hands to himself and she was full of encouragement. Eventually when they came downstairs more guests had arrived, so Rose was summoned by Charles to show them to their rooms. After being introduced she took them to where they were sleeping, all the time being the topic of conversation. Charles hadn't mentioned that he had such a beautiful sister, so now she was foremost in their thoughts, Charles was a distant second. "Lord Charles never told us he had such a beautiful sister," one of them said to Rose. "Charles would hardly notice he even had a sister," she replied without much compassion, and with that she left them. The local gentry were arriving and the mansion was starting to fill with guests. Mary was there to greet them as they arrived, as she knew most of them. They were infatuated — the men — by Mary's grace and beauty. The women were envious, such beauty, so wasted on the Irish. Why couldn't one of their sons sneer the daughter? She was as beautiful as her mother, they had to admit, and the sister of a lord ... what a prize! But apparently, she had opted for an Irish lad, in fact just a tenant farmer. What was she thinking?

Connor and Brendon felt very out of place in this congestion of upper-class gentry, so they wondered off outside to walk in the gardens. Connor expressed his thoughts about all this pomp and ceremony. "You know, Brendon, I will be happy when we leave all this behind, it is all false. The English have never accepted us Irish as people, but they take our money off us and think nothing of it. We actually work for them but we are still of lower class. I hate it. I'm so happy Rose found an Irishman and that we are going to be together again, somewhere where we are equal. Charles can have all this, it is where he belongs, he is of gentry standing." "I'm happy you feel this way about me and us Irish. I love Rose, she is such a caring person," said Brendon from the bottom of his heart. "You are all I wanted Joseph to be, Brendon, you are special to our family," he said with tears in his eyes. With these truths expressed they hugged each other. Just at this moment Charles happened to be looking out a window and saw his stepfather hugging Brendon and he felt livid, he never hugged him ... but why? This made him all the more determined to take Rose away from Brendon, to rid her of that bloody Irish tenant farmer. All his friends had expressed their feelings towards his sister; they were all professionals, this was the class of people that Rose belonged to. One friend in particular, a doctor, was truly smitten by Rose. He couldn't take his eyes off her, he had decided she was for him. He expressed his wish to Charles, who encouraged him to go for her.

All his friends thought his estate was fabulous and the gardens were commented on many times. Everyone was enjoying themselves as food and drinks were readily available. Mary was the perfect hostess, mixing with the gentry. This would be her final fling with them so she went all out to impress, because within a week she was going to become the enemy, perhaps even being branded as an Irish bitch. She was never short of admirers among the gentry but was the absolute envy of their wives. Rose was kept busy by Charles's friends who were all jostling for her attention. Connor and Brendon were in the stables watering and feeding the guests' horses, this is where they were more comfortable. Charles had the twins organised to hand hors d'oeuvre among the guests. Now it was time for the doctor to sort out Rose. He hadn't taken his eyes off her; she was the vision of an angel, one he would like to have hovering around him day and night. He asked her to walk around the gardens with him and tell him about the estate. Rose could see no harm in this so together they left the mansion and went out to the sunken rosebeds. He asked her who tended the gardens and when she told him it was all looked after by their mother, he was amazed. "Your mother is a beautiful lady, Charles is lucky to have her on his estate," he said. Rose pricked her ears. Did she hear right? But it wasn't his estate. She never said a word, she would just play along and see what else she would learn. "Yes, mother is a lovely lady, the gardens are her pride and joy," agreed Rose. "What do you do, Rose? You are as beautiful as your mother." "I am a teacher, I live in Ireland and teach at Dunmanway. I fell in love with the Irish people while on holiday so applied for a teaching position at a school there," she replied. "Why the Irish? Aren't the English more educated and wealthier than the Irish?" he asked. Rose told him, "Wealth doesn't bring happiness. Just to see the Irish enjoying life from the very little they have, that is happiness." What a simple being from such riches, he thought to himself. He just wanted to hold her in his arms and lay with her. "Actually, I have fallen in love with an Irishman, he is a tenant farmer with very little but he makes me happy," Rose told him. This knocked the doctor for a six; fancy such a beautiful specimen falling for a tenant farmer. He could offer her so much more. "But, Rose, you need more in life than just happiness. What about wealth?" he asked, hoping to persuade her otherwise. "I have seen what wealth can do to people and it is not pretty. My mother fell with an Irishman, then her life took a twist and she married Charles's father, Lord Albert Rothchild, but her love for the Irishman triumphed over all. I saw absolute love every day when I lived at home, wealth has nothing to do with it." He was stumped for words, never before had he heard feelings expressed with such sincerity. The words that came from Rose were as beautiful as she was. This made him want her all the more, she was rare indeed, a treasure that should belong to him. Suddenly she looked up and saw Brendon and waved for him to come down and join them. "This is my Brendon, meet one of Charles's friends," she said. Brendon shook his hand with a hearty shake and he felt the power this man possessed. "You have a lovely girl there, Brendon," he said. "Yes, she is my English rose, I love her dearly," and he put his arms around her and gently kiss her forehead. He then excused himself as he was helping Connor. "He is a very lucky man, Rose, how I envy him," he said, as he wanted to let her know how he felt. With this Rose suggested they walk back to the home. He was not ready to let her go, so he went and sorted out Lord Charles to see what he could arrange. The afternoon had come and gone and everyone was enjoying themselves.

It was now time for Charles to make his speech. He thanked everyone for coming to his estate and now that he had come of age he had some big plans for its future. "Thank you, mother, for your dedication to the grounds, they have drawn a lot of compliments, and thanks to the other members of my family for their help. I am now of age to join the gentry whom I will support. This may not have happened in the past but I can assure you that will change." With this announcement came cheers from the gentry. Mary took this on the chin but Connor and Rose were horrified. Fancy standing there saying this when he knew what his mother stood for. Rose looked around to see if she could see her mother, when she noticed the doctor she had been talking to staring at her. When she located her mother, she put her arms around her and told her she loved her. It was then she noticed the doctor standing beside her. "I meant what I said earlier, Rose. I could offer you more than just happiness," he said. "I'm sorry but I told you I already have a boyfriend whom I love dearly. Please leave me alone," and she walked away. By this time darkness had set in and she wanted to escape all the noise, so she walked down to the sunken gardens to reflect on the night. Next thing she was on the ground; she had been attacked from behind and someone was trying to climb on top of her. The attacker was kissing her brutally and trying to grope her. She wanted to scream but his mouth was on hers; panic set in. She fought him until she was able to let out a scream. With this she felt a terrible pain in her ear, then he was gone. Strangely enough the first person on the scene was Charles. "What's wrong, Rose?" he asked. "One of your friends attacked me," she sobbed. "My friends are all virile men, of course they are going to want you. Get over it, Rose, you weren't raped, nothing happened!" he said. Nothing happened? What was he talking about? She had been attacked! Was this acceptable behaviour among the upper-class? She was shocked. He was her brother, why was he not protecting her? "I hate you, Charles. I'm glad you're not my real brother." "What do you mean?" he asked. "Connor is my real father, not your father, you are only my half-brother," she told him in anger. His brain started working overtime; then if she wasn't his true sister, she would not be entitled to any of his father's estate.

It was then that Charles noticed her ear was bleeding profusely and blood was running down her neck. "Come with me, I will get my friend the doctor to have a look at it," he said. She followed him to the bathroom and sat until he returned with the doctor. He explained to him that Rose had been attacked. He looked at Rose's ear. "That is nasty, we will have to bathe it," he said as he lifted her hair away. He got a flannel and gently wiped the blood away, then he noticed it had run down her neck. "Undo your top buttons so I can bathe the blood from your neck," he asked of her. Rose did as she was told as she was still in shock. He could see the top of her breasts and gently brushed them as he wiped away the blood. She was so beautiful even after having been attacked. Rose was starting to feel a little uncomfortable, this he noticed, so told her to go to bed and rest, and he would have a look at it in the morning. Then Charles and he left. She was beside herself. Should she tell Brendon? No, he would want revenge in a big way, as would her father. She decided to hide it with her hair until tomorrow when the celebrations were over. She went to her room and undressed then got into bed. Her ear was throbbing. Brendon was looking for Rose everywhere but someone had seen her going up the stairs. He walked into the room only to find her sound asleep. He undressed and climbed in beside her.

The next morning when Rose woke there was blood all over her pillow and her ear was throbbing. She quickly turned her pillow over so as to hide it from Brendon. She quietly climbed out of bed and bathed the blood from her ear and her hair, then brushed it so no-one saw her ear. It was only now that last night came flooding back. Who was her attacker, why, and Charles reaction? Did he think it was okay for one of his friends to try to rape her? Then she remembered what she had told him. None of this was meant to be revealed. Would he forget what she had said? Unlikely! She went to the parlour and found her mother getting the last of the guests their breakfasts, as it was an early start back for them. She offered to help, wondering which of them might have been her attacker. When they had finished Mary went to give Rose a hug when she noticed her ear. "Rose, what happened?" she asked in shock. Rose told her about last night and they both burst into tears. "What did Brendon say?" Rose hadn't told him and didn't want him to know until the guests had left as there would be big trouble and she didn't know who the attacker was. Brendon would have no mercy on any of Charles's guests. Then she had to tell her mother what she had said to Charles last night in anger. "I told him I hated him, it was as if it was acceptable behaviour to him, he told me to get over it, that nothing had happened, but something did happen, mother! I told him I was glad I was only his half-sister. I'm sorry but I was so angry." "Come here, my darling, he was lucky that was all you said." She lifted Rose's hair back and couldn't believe her ear had been bitten right through and it was all bruised. "We will have to get you to a doctor," said a concerned Mary. "It's all right mother, one of Charles's friends is a doctor. He attended to it last night, he said he will have a look at it this morning." With this she pulled her hair over her ear.

Rose waited by the door for the doctor, as he had packed his bags and was getting his carriage ready to leave. He called Rose over to have a look at her wound. He lifted her hair back, he wanted to kiss her neck, but he saw her mother watching. Sadly, this angel could never be his as she was already claimed. He bathed her ear to make sure there was no infection. "You will be left with a scar, Rose," then he whispered in her ear. "Each morning when you look in the mirror you will remember me, Rose, you will never forget me, this will be a reminder." Then he climbed on his carriage and drove off. Rose just stood there. What did he mean? She couldn't work it out. No, it couldn't be what she was thinking, surely, he wasn't the person that did this to her, not a doctor? But as she slowly worked out the meaning of his words, it all became clear. She ran down the driveway calling to him, "You bastard, I hate you." Mary heard her yelling so ran to her. "What is wrong, Rose?" "It was him, mother, it was the doctor," she sobbed. Connor heard the commotion and came running from the stables. Mary pulled Rose's hair back and showed him her ear, then she told him about the attack last night. They had just worked out who her attacker was: the doctor. With this Connor ran to the stables and jumped on the buggy and down the road he went; he was going to kill him.

By now Brendon had surfaced and as he came the stairs he noticed Rose in her mother's arms. He could see she was in tears. "What happened?" he asked. She ran into his arms. She couldn't tell him. Mary relayed to Brendon what had taken place last night, and it was only a few minutes ago that they learned who her attacker was. When he saw her ear, he was furious. His poor Rose, why would someone want to hurt her? Revenge was first and foremost on his mind. Mary told him Connor was away trying to find him. "Where is Charles?" he demanded. "Did I hear my name mentioned?" said Charles as he came into the room. Brendon let go of Rose and grabbed Charles by his collar. "You should be more careful who you invite onto this estate. Some of your friends are no more than savages." "Get off me, you are a nobody, you are on my property. Don't tell me who I can bring home!" he roared at Brendon. "One of your so-called colleagues attacked Rose and bit her ear. He tried to rape her, what a mongrel, what have you got to say about that?" yelled Brendon as he tightened his grip on Charles's shirt. "He was infatuated by Rose, he wanted her." "That does not give him the right to touch her, you knew she belonged to me. Why didn't you tell him?" asked Brendon. "I told him to go for it, he can offer her more than a poor Irish tenant farmer." With that Brendon let fly with his fist and Charles fell to the floor. Just at that moment Connor appeared on the scene and saw Charles lying in a heap. "Thank you, Brendon, you saved me a job," then he turned to Charles. "You're a mongrel, Charles, you didn't even have the decency to protect your sister." Charles picked himself up. "She is only my half-sister. I will see she gets nothing from father's estate now that I know this," he retaliated. An upset Mary said, "We are talking about one of your friends trying to rape your sister and all you can think about is the estate. Your father would turn in his grave. You have disgraced yourself, Charles, leave this room." With this he left. "That lad is going to get what he deserves later this week," said Connor. "I can't wait to see him knocked off his pedestal, revenge will be sweet."

"What are we going to do about you, Rose, you have been through so much. Do you want us to report this incident to the authorities?" asked Connor. "No, father. I trusted that doctor, to think he could do that, then tell me every time I looked in the mirror I would remember him by my scars, that is so sick. Let us all go for a walk together past the rose gardens." This they did, with Rose shedding a tear; this was closure for her.

13

The Rude Awakening

No-one saw Charles for the rest of the day; he had made himself scarce. Mary and Rose stripped the guests' rooms and as Rose took the sheets off one bed she found a letter that was addressed to her under a pillow. She hesitated. Would she open it or destroy it, but then she would wonder forever what was in it. She sat on the bed with the envelope in her hand. She plucked up courage to open it, and as she started reading she felt her heart sink. Surely this wasn't true! She quickly shredded it into tiny pieces and put it in the rubbish. This was better forgotten and not be revealed to anyone. It would only split the family further apart, there was enough damage done now. Rose could live with this secret, no-one else could, so it was better buried right here!

Tonight was the last supper they would all have together

at the estate, as Rose and Brendon were leaving in the morning. They would not be back to the estate before the family moved to Ireland. Rose had mixed emotions. If Charles was taken out of the equation, then her memories would have been happy ones, but how things had changed! Everyone was ready to move in a new direction, especially Connor. He had little or no time whatsoever for Charles, as he had treated him with contempt and this was coming between him and Mary. Mary still felt however horrid Charles was, she was his mother and he was Albert's child. If not for Albert none of this would have been possible. She had a lot to remember him for; he ended her life of poverty, replacing it with a life of plenty. Mary went to Charles's room and asked him to come down and have supper with them as Rose was leaving tomorrow. They did not wait for him, they began to eat, but he did arrive. He was very quiet, but he had at least joined them, for this Mary was thankful. This would be the last time they would be together as a family at this table.

Mary stood up and thanked everyone for pulling together and helping make yesterday the special day it was for Charles's coming of age party. "I hope you recognise this, Charles?" He stood up and acknowledged with a thank you. "Next week there will be some changes on the estate. I am hiring a butler for my personal needs, just as father had. He will be here full time and will require a room in my wing. I am moving into father's room, so this wing will be out of bounds to the rest of the family. I am going out for the night, so will say goodbye to you, Rose," and with this he left. They all sat staring at each other, they were lost for words. He hadn't even acknowledged Brendon. Connor was the first to speak. "I'm sorry for Charles's behaviour, Brendon, but we all know what he is like. With his speech tonight, it will make it easier for us all to walk off the estate. He is going to surround himself with staff, all whom will address him as Lord Charles, which he will love, as he will look important in the eyes of the gentry. I'm sorry, Mary, my love, you must feel heartbroken with all that has happened?" he asked. "My heart has been broken, yes, not for Charles, but for Rose. She will leave here with memories that will haunt her for forever. For this to happen on her last visit home is disgraceful. I thought I would be sad to say goodbye to my life here but no, it is time to go. I will always remember Albert, he has provided well for all of us, but Charles is another matter. His father would be bitterly disappointed in him, this I know in my own heart. Albert was a good man. Charles will find the life he deserves here, after all it is his heritage, he is the only one who legally has a right to the estate." "But what about Rose, she is his sister?" asked the twins. The time had come! "Rose is your blood sister, Connor is her father, she is only a half-sister to Charles. No-one knew this and Charles only found out yesterday," said Mary. The twins ran to Rose and hugged her. There were tears all round. That was all the secrets out in the open, except for the one Rose was harbouring!

The home was empty again apart from the twins. Rose and Brendon had left yesterday and Charles didn't came home again last night. But unbeknown to Mary, Charles had gone to her solicitor to see how Albert's will was worded. Now that he knew Rose was not his father's daughter, this meant he was entitled to half the estate, the same share as his mother, then he could override her with his peerage, this giving him the upper hand. But there was a big disappointment awaiting him, because in the will, Rose was named as a beneficiary along with Joseph and

Charles. If Albert had left his children unnamed, then this would have a very different outcome. When told this by the estate solicitor he was bitterly disappointed, as his imagined power had not materialised. He asked the solicitor to arrange a meeting time for his mother and he to meet over his position with the estate, now that he was of age. The date was set down for Thursday at ten o'clock. The solicitor would call and see Mary at the estate and let her know about these arrangements. He could have left it to Charles, but he had a couple of points he wanted to discuss with her before the meeting.

That night at the estate when Charles turned up for supper, Mary attacked him over his blatant disregard for Rose's Brendon. "You were so rude, Charles, he is Rose's fiancé and a lovely person, he will look after Rose. Why do you treat people like that?" "Rose deserves better than a tenant farmer, a nobody. She could have had any of my upper-class friends, they all liked her," he answered. A hostile Connor said, "You would entrust your sister to those scum of the earth, look what happened to her. Brendon would never harm her. There is such a thing as respect, Charles, but you haven't learnt this yet." "I can tell you he won't be a tenant farmer for long, I will make sure of that. I will put him off the land, then Rose will come crawling back," replied a pompous Charles. This was too much for Connor. He went around and cuffed Charles under the ears. "And you, you won't be here for much longer, I will have you evicted off my estate!" he yelled at Connor as he left the room. The twins witnessed this and burst into tears. Here was their father being told he would have to leave. Mary went to them and hugged them both, and asked them to go to their room, that it would be all sorted out tomorrow, which was Thursday. She took

Connor by the hand and led him upstairs to their room where they lay on the bed in each other's arms. Who would have thought it would all come to this? A sword had pierced Mary's heart and blood was about to be spilt. Tomorrow it would run hot!

Today was Thursday. The twins went to school this morning knowing what was about to take place at the solicitor's. Connor was worried for Mary so he drove her into town and would wait and pick her up after the meeting. No-one knew how revengeful Charles might be when he learnt what he was about to be told. As Mary walked into the solicitor's she saw Charles coming from his office. She hurried so she didn't have to face him. They sat on a chair beside each other, opposite the solicitor. He explained Albert's will to them: Mary owned half the estate, and the other half was divided between Rose and Charles, now that Joseph was gone. Of course, the peerage went to Charles; he became Lord Charles Rothchild. "What has happened, Charles, your mother has taken ten Irish farms out of the estate and you are left with eight Irish farms. In your mother's ten farms, one has been allocated to Rose as her share. You will retain the English estate outright." Charles could not believe what he had just been told. How could his mother do this? "But she can't do this, how am I meant to survive? I need all the farms to keep the estate going." He turned to his mother with hatred in his eyes. "This was my father's family estate, how can you do this to him? You were nothing until you met father, now you are taking from me what is rightfully mine!" he yelled.

"Charles, your father chose me, he looked after me, I in return looked after him. He left me a letter which the solicitor gave me to say I could do what I liked with my share. He even suggested I looked after the Irish tenant farmers and this is what I intend to do. He never really understood the plight of the Irish until he met me, and when I told him my mother died of starvation because there wasn't enough food for her family so she went without, he was devastated. The gentry have never known or cared about the Irish, and when I heard you say you would side with the gentry and vote against me, then I decided to take these measures to secure the lives of at least some of the tenant farmers. What you and the gentry do is your business, but the wheat from my farms will not be crossing the Irish Sea, it will stay in Ireland. The gentry will hate me, but I was just someone they all wanted to bed. They had no principles or respect for your father. You will have to manage the estate with your eight farms plus your income from elsewhere. All is not lost, Charles, but you have been brought down to size. That you would take from your sister her fiancé's farm was the end for me, especially after what you have put her through. You are a spoilt child who needs to be taught the hard facts of life, so this is it, Charles, lesson number one," said an empty-hearted Mary.

Charles was bewildered by all of this. Now he only had eight farms, he could not pull rank over the gentry; he would just be one of them but with a title. He asked to see the finances and when they were presented to him and he saw the amount in the account, he was ropable. "Where are all the profits for all the years since father's death?" he asked. "They were your mother's. You only have claim from the day you turned twenty-one. I think your mother has been very fair with the amount she has left there for you," replied the solicitor. With this Charles he got up from his seat and stalked out of the office. "That went well?" remarked the solicitor. This was not the life Charles imagined for himself — it was all meant to end in bright lights and plenty of bubbles! The solicitor took Mary's hand. "You can expect retaliations from him when it all sinks in. Leave the estate, Mary, and find a new life in Ireland. He will never forgive you; you deserve better. As you say the gentry will hate you for this, so expect hostile words from them, but I know in my own mind you will find the right answers." Mary thanked the solicitor and left his office, only to find Connor waiting outside the door for her, as he had seen Charles stalking back to his office. Who would be next to suffer?

Mary explained to the children that things might be said at school when this gossip hit the gentry, but it would probably not happen for a couple of days. They were to tell her if this happened sooner. They had word that their new home in Ireland was nearly completed, about another two weeks. Rose and Brendon were in charge, so this was good news. It meant they would only have to endure here for another two weeks! They were taking nothing from the estate, just their personal items. It would be a fresh start and the Irish shopkeepers would benefit from their spending. Everyone was prepared for an onslaught of anger from all angles, but it would only be for a short time. No-one other than themselves knew they were leaving the estate, this was their secret.

Two days had passed and there was still no sign of Charles at the estate, but two letters had been delivered this morning. They were left at the front entrance door, both addressed to Mary. She opened the first one to find the gentry had called a board meeting on Thursday at her estate at two o'clock. The second letter stated they had exactly one month to leave the estate and they were not to remove any of the estate chattels. They were to take their personal possessions only and leave by the end of the month. This was no surprise! When the twins came home from school they were not happy as they had been teased, being called Irish paupers, which had hurt them. So the gossip had started. That would be why a board meeting was called. But what would be the relevance of a meeting? There was nothing to discuss, now that she was the enemy.

That evening while they were having supper, Charles walked in and stood at the door. "I want everything cleared out of father's wing tomorrow, this will out of bounds from then on. My butler is shifting in on Friday and he will have a room in my wing. He is my private butler and will not perform duties for anyone else other than me. I am saddened, mother, with what you have done. Father provided well for you and your Irish brood. You used him to make a better life for yourselves, you never really fitted in, you weren't of gentry breed. It was only because of your good looks that you were noticed. That was probably why father fell for you, but in the end, you are only of Irish stock, so are your children and their father. I can't change anything now, you have beat me, but I will rise again," he said. "I'm pleased for you, Charles. How sad for you to know you were bred from Irish blood mixed with English blood, thus making you part Irish. Sadly, the English greed outweighed the Irish passion in your genes, but you are right, I have beat you. Fancy an Irishwoman putting one over an Englishman. One day you will look back on your life, Charles. You might realise because you were a baby when your father died, that someone stepped into his shoes and filled his role for nearly twenty years. Yet you hardly acknowledge him, how ungrateful is that, but never mind, we as a family will never be on our own. We will look after each other, that is what us Irish do," Mary said in a very calm voice. "Who was Joseph's father, mother? Did you go behind father's back?" "That is no business of yours, Charles. Tell me what really did happened that day with the gun," she asked. "I fired the gun, the peerage belonged to me, not him." With this a cry of agony rang out from the table and Connor fell to the floor. Mary ran to him to hold and comfort him. He was sobbing like a baby; his Joseph had died needlessly, he was never in line for the peerage. "I will shift back in on Friday night," said Charles, and left.

Mary walked Connor to their room. He was devastated, although he knew in his own heart this is what may have happened, but to be told so coldly without a smidgen of remorse, nothing had prepared him for this. He didn't want to talk to Mary, he just wanted to be on his own to finish his mourning for Joseph. He didn't want to be on the estate any more; he was ready to leave right now. The heartache was too great, but worse, he was frightened what he would do to Charles when he saw him again. Mary left Connor to attend to the twins. They were hugging each other crying their hearts out; what they had just witnessed had devastated them. They clung to their mother. "Let us go tomorrow, mother, we have to get father away, he shouldn't have to see Charles again. Please can we be away by Friday?" they pleaded.

The twins took the cart to school the next day but they arrived back at the estate at lunch time. The kids at school were now pulling their hair; this was the end for Mary. Connor was unhappy and their children were being punished simply because they were Irish. It had all come to an end, no more was anyone going to suffer. They held a family meeting and it was decided that Connor and the twins would leave the very next day with their belongings and begin their journey across the Irish Sea to Ireland. Mary would follow in a couple of days as she had final papers to sign at the solicitors. She would take them to the train station early tomorrow morning so they could catch the first train. Connor worried about Mary staying but it was important to get the twins away from all this. How much more could they take? The afternoon was spent packing. They would pack their clothes and only the things that were important to them, as they were limited to what they could manage. Not that it mattered much, they didn't want too many reminders of their lives on the estate, especially in these later years. The good memories they would store in their minds. They were excited knowing the teasing would be finished and they were leaving Charles behind. No-one at school would know they were gone. That night Mary and Connor lay in each other's arms. They would miss one another but the excitement of a new life would bring back the happiness that had escaped them lately. Connor stroked Mary's hair and kissed her neck, then whispered in her ear. His hands caressed her upper body then gently slid down her back to where he could pull her body close to his. Mary responded by clutching his buttocks and bringing him hard against her so she could feel his manly parts ready to take her. This would be their last lovemaking session in this bed, so they wanted it to be something special. Mary clung to Connor all night. She hoped his enthusiasm for life would come back in a new environment away from Charles.

There was great excitement as the bags were being loaded into the carriage. They would put them inside instead of on top, then no-one would see what was happening. The boys would sit up front with their father and Mary would ride inside. They weren't sure if their home was finished but they would stay at an inn in Dunmanway until it was completed. Rose and Brendon's cottage was too small for them, besides Rose would be teaching all day. They couldn't let her know they were arriving, as it happened so quickly. At the train station they hugged each other. "Take care, my darling," Connor told Mary, as he worried about Charles and his hostilities. The boys told their mother to hurry back to them as they would miss her. They loaded their luggage onto the train, then the whistle blew, and it was time for them to start their journey.

Mary drove the carriage back to the estate. She would spend the next few days sorting out what was left of the twins' bits and pieces and have a big fire. She would pack her personal belongings and burn all that was not needed. She cleaned out Albert's wing of the mansion as instructed by Charles as tomorrow she had the gentry board meeting, then Charles would move in on Friday. The same day as his butler. This time there would be no drinks or hors d'oeuvre after the meeting, that would be it. She didn't know if he would be attending or not, she would just have to wait and see. Because the twins never turned up at school, one of the teachers came to the estate to see why. Mary politely told him they no longer lived on the estate. He was taken by surprise. Nothing had been said to the contrary so why wasn't anyone told? "The twins were being picked on by the other students because of their Irish heritage. Nothing was done about it, they had had enough and so had I. As a result of this, they have now moved away," said an upset Mary. The schoolteacher was shocked as the Rothchilds had supported the school and the daughter Rose taught there. He apologised to Mary. "I would have thought the English would be more accepting of Irish students, but this apparently is not the case, not in this wealthy area, which is sad." Mary let him know how she felt. On this note he left.

She rode into town to have her final meeting with the estate solicitor. He told her all the estate business had been removed from his office to Charles's office across town. Charles told him he was handling his estate himself so he would no longer be required. Mary signed the last papers pertaining to the ownership of all her Irish farms, now everything was final. She told him Connor and the boys had left and she would be following in a couple of days. He shook her hand and wished her well. "You are a good businesswoman, Mary. I know you will look after your tenant farmers, but of course that is what you Irish people do, you look after your own. I know you will do well," he said as he bade her farewell. Mary had one last favour to ask from him. When she caught the train on Saturday morning, could he see that the carriage was returned to the estate, as Charles didn't know she was leaving.

It was two o'clock on Thursday and the gentry carriages were arriving at the estate. Mary had set the boardroom up for the meeting. As they arrived she told them to tether their horses to the rails themselves. "Where is Connor today?" they asked, as this was usually his job. "He's not here today," she replied. Then she saw Charles pull up. He spoke politely to her and walked to the boardroom. The first part of the meeting was for the gentry only. She would be asked to attend when they were ready for her, which made her a little annoyed. Had Charles arranged this? She waited in the drawing room until she was summoned. When they were ready for her, she was asked by the chairperson to sit up front beside him, as there were going to be questions asked. He started the ball rolling. "Mary, we have heard that you have split Albert's estate by removing some of the farms. Is this true?" "Yes, gentlemen, that is true, but it is really none of your business. What goes on on our estate has no relevance to anyone other than members of our family." "Albert was a dear friend as well as a business partner, but we feel you have gone behind his back, Mary," he replied. "But many of you went behind Albert's back," she answered. "What do you mean, Mary?" "I can look around this room and see at least eight gentry who tried their best to bed me behind Albert's back, even within days of his passing. This to me is not a friendship, but then I am Irish, I don't understand how the cold-blooded English conduct friendships. Albert was a good man." This brought a deadly silence to the boardroom. Charles was in shock, he couldn't believe what his mother had just said. "Are you in with us on the importing of the wheat?" someone asked. "No, gentlemen, none of my wheat will be crossing the Irish Sea, it will remain in Ireland," Mary replied. "But you can't do that, we need your yield to help keep our importing costs to a minimum." "I am sorry, gentlemen of the gentry, you are on your own. As you all know, I care deeply for the Irish, for they have suffered. If I can save but a few tenant farmers, then that is what I will do." "What about your son? You have done him wrong," someone called out from the room. "Charles is a big boy, in fact a spoilt one at that, but his ego will indeed see him through. The estate is now his and as a lord he has it all. Any more questions, gentlemen?" Mary asked. No-one said a word. "Then I will take my leave. There will be no drinks or hors d'oeuvre today," and with this she left the boardroom for the last time. This would give them something to think about, she thought to herself.

Mary went back to the home to continue with her packing; only one more day and she would be gone. But the silence didn't last for long. Through the entrance she heard her name being called. She came down the stairs and there stood Charles in a rage. "What a bitch you are, mother, I am ashamed of you. Fancy making a fool of yourself in front of the gentry!" he screamed. "The only fools in the room were the gentry and yourself, Charles. What a shallow lot of upper-class spineless creatures you are. No-one stood up to me, but then they are not used to being spoken to by a hot-headed Irishwoman. I think I did well." Charles came at Mary and slapped her hard across the face. "Your father would hate you for this, Charles," she said as she walked away in tears.

She only had Friday to spend on the Rothchild estate. All the joy that once lived here had been replaced by hatred. What would Albert have thought? He would be sad to know his Irish rose was leaving, but deep down he would be understanding of her plight. His son was so different to him; Albert was a gentle soul, but Charles was cold-blooded and selfish. Charles hated her and she couldn't feel much more for him. What had happened? she asked herself as tears streamed down her face. Such a beautiful place, but now even the gardens harboured unpleasant memories, but the tool-shed was where the downhill slide started. Soon it would all be over. Later in the afternoon she saw Charles pull up in his carriage. He had someone with him. It must be the butler, she thought. She watched from her bedroom window. The gentleman was young, about Charles's age. No, that must a friend, she thought. She carried on with her packing. Later she was disturbed by a knock on the door. "It's me, mother, will you be coming down for supper? asked Charles. "No, thank you, not tonight. I'm tired, I'm going to bed." She waited for the apology, but it was not forthcoming. Later in the night she made her way down the stairs to get a glass of water. As she passed the drawing room she could hear laughter so she stopped and peeped in. There sitting in the settee was Charles and the young man with their arms around each other. She backed off and stole back up the stairs without her drink, but in total shock. Surely not, no, it wasn't true! Her head was spinning. Just when she thought nothing else could go wrong, she was faced with this! But no, she was reading something into a situation that was innocent, she told herself, and that was what she wanted to believe.

Mary was up early this morning and had loaded all her bags into the carriage, when she heard someone speaking to her. She looked around and there was the young man. "Good morning, ma'am, pleased to meet you. I am George, Lord Charles's new butler." "Hello, George," she said. My God, so he was the butler, thank goodness. That would explain what she had seen last night; perhaps they were celebrating. All the horrible thoughts from last night quickly vanished. As she was about to climb onto the carriage Charles appeared. "You're up and away early, mother, where is everyone? The home is so quiet," he said. "It is Saturday, they are all still in bed," said a startled Mary. "Where are you going so early?" "I have an appointment, I must go," she said and away she went. When she reached the train station the solicitor was waiting for her. He lifted her bags down and put them on the platform, so all she had to do was lift them onto the train when it arrived. He was fond of Mary and was sad to see her go. "I will write and keep in touch with any news from the estate. Goodbye, Mary, and take care," he told her as he shook her hand. He walked to the carriage and took the reins and off he went. A friend was following him to bring him back when he had delivered the carriage to the estate.

As he pulled up outside the front entrance, Charles appeared on the scene. "Where is mother?" he asked. "Your family have gone, Charles. Your mother said to say goodbye." "What do you mean they have gone?" he asked. "Your brothers and Connor left two days ago and your mother is on the train at this very moment." "But they never said goodbye, where have they gone?" he asked. "Your mother told me not to say of their whereabouts." "But I never apologised for hitting her," he sobbed. "Perhaps that is why she didn't want you to know where she has gone. What sort of man would hit his mother? You have lost a loved one you will never replace, Charles. Your mother is one of the nicest people I have known and is a very intelligent woman, she deserves happiness," he replied. Charles stood and cried like a baby; it was only now he realised he was alone.

14

Going Home to Ireland

Mary was reunited with her family and they had moved into their new home. It wasn't the mansion they had left behind, but by Irish standards it was a very large home. The boys loved going to college each day, the students were friendly, but the best thing of all they looked like any other student; they didn't look different, and there was no more teasing. Connor had the builders back building his dream workshop, passion had come back in his life and he was happy once again. In a month's time Rose and Brendon were getting married so this was creating a lot of excitement. Mary had fun shopping for items for her new home and the local shopkeepers all smiled when they saw her come into town. She was known to spend money so everyone welcomed her, she was their friend. When she looked back on her life on the estate, other than Albert and the gentry men along with the solicitor, no-one had bothered with her because she was Irish. None of the women wanted to befriend her for fear of their husbands straying, which was known to happen among the gentry. Well did Mary know about this ... most had tried!

Mary had sent out letters to her tenant farmers to let them know that the ownership of their lands had changed. Instead of the Rothchild estate owning the farms, they had been taken over by the O'Leary estate, which was based in Ireland. No longer did they have absentee English landlords. The new landlords were going to retain the wheat in Ireland; it would not be crossing the Irish Sea as it always had done, and this was a new start for everyone. If they received good prices for their wheat, now that there were no export taxes, then the profit would come back to the tenant farmers by way of a bonus. This was unheard of; no landlords ever passed any profits on to the tenant farmers. She said she would try to meet them but if there were any problems to please get in touch with her. But there were never problems if the farmers were treated right; they were grateful to have the farms to make a living from. She had earmarked two farms for the twins but that was a couple of years away so they were still farmed by tenant farmers. She and Connor built their home on a smaller farm which could be split at a later date between the two boys' future farms. Mary was busy setting out her lawns and gardens. She never thought back to what she left behind; those memories had faded. It had all ended in tears and heartache. This was a chance of a new beginning in her beloved homeland.

Today Rose was getting married. Daniel and his family had arrived down from Dundalk and were staying with Mary and Connor. Patrick and his family lived near and they all gathered at Mary's home. Their children were part of the bridal party; the two little girls were flower girls and the little boy was the pageboy. These were the ratbags that told their headmaster that their Aunty Rose was going to marry Brendon because they had seen them kissing. Rose looked beautiful in her wedding dress. She was a beauty before the dress even went on, but this was something else. They all took carriages to the little Dunmanway church. Rose chose this church because her brother Joseph's service was held here, as was her grandfather's, so it was a choice based on sentimental reasons. Brendon's family were already at the church. Connor was the proudest father as he walked his beautiful daughter down the aisle, while Mary and the twins were seated in the front pew. The littlies trailed behind staring all around and giggling. They had the guests smiling; it all added a bit of humour. Brendon was the happiest man alive. At last Rose was going to belong to him, and when he saw her in her wedding dress he couldn't hold back his tears. She was his princess, his beautiful English rose. He just wanted to take her in his arms, but that would have to wait; first the formalities. When they were announced as man and wife, he took Rose into his arms and held her close then kissed her. The children laughed and pointed to Rose and Brendon. They knew two years ago that they were going to marry, they had told the headmaster so! Rose was no longer Rose Rothchild, she was now Mrs Carey. She was happy about the name change!

After the marriage ceremony had finished, the wedding party and relatives walked outside into the churchyard and lay a rose by their father James Nyhan's headstone and then by Rose's brother Joseph O'Leary's headstone. On this special day they were not forgotten; they were part of the wedding celebrations.

All the guests came back to Mary's home for the wedding breakfast. It had been organised by a local women's club to whom Mary had given a generous donation, any way to help make these people's lives more joyful. After the speeches Mary made a special announcement. "To Rose and Brendon, as a gift to you both from the Rothchild estate, which Rose was left a share, here are the deeds to your farm. You are no longer a tenant farmer, Brendon; you and Rose are now landowners. Poor Brendon, he couldn't control his tears. Never in a million years did he ever think he would be a landowner. He had dreamt about it many times but for it to happen was unbelievable. "Mary and Connor, thank you so much. Two dreams have been fulfilled today: I wed my English rose, and now we own our farm. The third dream hopefully will not be too far away and it will have two little feet and keep us awake at night." This brought cheers and laughter from all. "I hope your homemade bed will stand up to the pounding it will get tonight," whispered Rose to Brendon. "I told you it was made for a good working out," he whispered back. There was one more surprise. "Rose, I have our wedding present to you. Here is an amount of money from the estate that has been put aside for you from the day you turned twenty-one," and Mary handed her a bank account. Rose was shocked at the amount; it would mean they could buy more land or make their cottage larger. She hugged her mother and father and was forever grateful, as was Brendon.

A year had passed and Connor's workshop was in business. The neighbouring farmers as well as the townspeople who wanted anything fixed, all came to see

Connor. He was Mr Fixit! He was a happy soul again; for the first time in many years he was able to provide for his family. If he felt he wanted to escape, he would be found down at the churchyard talking to his beloved Joseph. He was so happy they made the decision to have him buried back here in Ireland, it made it a little easier for him to bear. Mary had joined several clubs and loved meeting with the Irish women, they were the 'pure essence of life'. Their pain and laughter was shared among them all, but what Mary loved most, like her sons, she was just one of them. She would hold garden parties and have an open invite to all who wanted to attend, and they would arrive dressed in their Sunday best and laughter would ring out around the countryside of Curraghnaloughra bringing it alive. Mary realised this is what she had missed in her life, not having had the company of other women.

For all Mary's wealth, this was the happiest time of her life, back here in Ireland where her life had begun nearly fifty years ago. These were her people, this was her life and she still had her hot-blooded Irishman. He had been on this journey with her and they had both suffered along the way, but their passion for each other had held them together through all their ups and downs.

One day while Mary and Rose were reminiscing on some of the good times they had on the estate, Mary mentioned about her last day there when she had met Charles's butler. She was surprised that he was so young, as her idea of a butler was an older man. Then she told Rose what she had seen that night, Charles and a young man with their arms around each other. "You know, Rose, a sickening feeling came over me. I didn't want to believe what my mind was telling me, but thankfully the next morning he introduced himself as Lord Charles's new butler. I was relieved, they were probably celebrating. I couldn't have lived with the other thought that came to my mind, it would have been the end of me."

Rose took her mother's hand. "That life is over, mother, we are a happy family once again, don't let us go back there," and she knew the secret that she had been harbouring would never be released, as she now knew it would destroy her mother. Charles had brought her enough pain, she didn't deserve to suffer any more. But now Rose understood why Charles thought the way he did when one of his friends attacked her, and why he said to forget it, nothing had happened! Was he part of it? He held no sympathy for the opposite sex, they meant nothing, there were only two people in his life ... Charles and his young butler!

Rose and Brendon were starting the next generation as Rose had just announced that she was with child. This was the beginning of another era that would give this new generation the choice to settle in Ireland, their homeland, and not be forced to leave like their great-grandparents. Those days of poverty were a distant memory to Mary and Connor, but they would never be completely forgotten, for this was what had sent Mary on her journey to find a better life. One that would steer her family away from that dreaded word, the word she never wanted to hear ever again ... starvation!

All this word brought was tears to Mary's eyes and sad memories of her mother, a mother who had sacrificed her own life, to help save the lives of those she loved dearly ... her own children.

About the Author

Margaret Nyhon lives in Alexandra, in the Central Otago province of New Zealand, where she writes, paints and practises the crafts of printing and bookbinding. She has worked extensively in hospitality management in New Zealand and resort management in Australia. The urge to trace her family history led her to the writing of her first non-fiction work, *de Marisco*. She has since written several fiction and non-fiction works. Margaret is married and has three adult children and two grandsons.

Other Books by the Author

Non-fiction

de Marisco
Freedom Knows No Boundaries
A Wake-up Call
A Shattered Dream Across the Tasman

Fiction

Isobella (Book 1 in the *Isobella* series)
Isobella: Self Redemption (Book 2 in the *Isobella* series)
Papa's Girl Emmeline
Betrayal by an Irish Rose

Coming Soon

Pimchan's Journey Away From Poverty
Based on a true story